Roxie and the
Red Rose Mystery

Other Crossway Books by
Hilda Stahl

THE SADIE ROSE ADVENTURE SERIES
Sadie Rose and the Daring Escape
Sadie Rose and the Cottonwood Creek Orphan
Sadie Rose and the Outlaw Rustlers
Sadie Rose and the Double Secret
Sadie Rose and the Mad Fortune Hunters
Sadie Rose and the Phantom Warrior
Sadie Rose and the Champion Sharpshooter
Sadie Rose and the Secret Romance
Sadie Rose and the Impossible Birthday Wish

GROWING UP ADVENTURES
Sendi Lee Mason and the Milk Carton Kids
Sendi Lee Mason and the Stray Striped Cat
Sendi Lee Mason and the Big Mistake
Sendi Lee Mason and the Great Crusade

KAYLA O'BRIAN ADVENTURES
Kayla O'Brian and the Dangerous Journey
Kayla O'Brian: Trouble at Bitter Creek Ranch
Kayla O'Brian and the Runaway Orphans

DAISY PUNKIN
Meet Daisy Punkin
The Bratty Brother

BEST FRIENDS
#1: Chelsea and the Outrageous Phone Bill
#2: Big Trouble for Roxie
#3: Kathy's Baby-sitting Hassle
#4: Hannah and the Special 4th of July
#6: Kathy's New Brother
#7: A Made-over Chelsea
#8: No Friends for Hannah

#5

Roxie and the Red Rose Mystery

Hilda Stahl

CROSSWAY BOOKS • WHEATON, ILLINOIS
A DIVISION OF GOOD NEWS PUBLISHERS

Roxie and the Red Rose Mystery.

Copyright © 1992 by Word Spinners, Inc.

Published by Crossway Books, a division of
Good News Publishers, 1300 Crescent Street, Wheaton, Illinois 60187.

Cover illustration: Paul Casale

First printing, 1992

Printed in the United States of America

Library of Congress Cataloging-in-Publication Data
Stahl, Hilda.
   Roxie and the red rose mystery / by Hilda Stahl.
      p.   cm. — (Best friends : #5)
    Summary: Twelve-year-old Roxie needs the support of her best
friends and God when she starts helping Mary Harland with her entry in
the local art contest and falls in love with Mary's older brother Dan.
   [1. Artists—Fiction. 2. Contests—Fiction. 3. Friendship—
Fiction. 4. Christian life—Fiction.] I. Title. II. Series: Stahl,
Hilda. Best friends : #5.
PZ7.S78244Ro 1992   [Fic]—dc20   92-4851
ISBN 0-89107-681-6

---

00   99   98   97
15   14   13   12   11   10   9   8   7   6   5

Dedicated with love to
Jamie L. Smith

Contents

1

The Good Deed

Roxie sank back against the tree in her front yard as she listened to Chelsea McCrea. Hannah Shigwam and Kathy Aber, the other Best Friends, sat in a circle and listened as if they loved every word Chelsea was saying.

"Mary Harland and her family definitely need help," Chelsea said in her soft Oklahoma accent as she pushed back her long red hair. "And as members of the Best Friends Club and members of the *King's Kids* we promised to do good deeds."

Roxie bit back a groan. *She* had never liked the idea of doing good deeds as much as the others had, but she'd gone along with it just to make them happy. Now they wanted to help Mary Harland and her family. Of all the people they could choose to help . . . ! Mary Harland was nice and all, but she lived in the poor section of Middle Lake. Roxie, Chelsea, and Hannah lived in a new subdivision in really nice homes, and Kathy lived across the street in an older section of town, but still a nice home. Mary Harland sometimes even *looked* poor when she came to Sunday school.

Chelsea solemnly studied the Best Friends. "Hannah's dad checked out the area where the Harlands live and checked out the family. The area doesn't have violence or drugs, and the family is okay, so it's safe for us to go there." Chelsea pointed to the others. "It's time to take a vote. Raise your hand if you vote yes."

Hannah, Kathy, and Chelsea raised their hands. Roxie sat on hers. The three girls looked right at Roxie. "Well?" they said all together.

Roxie bit her lower lip and narrowed her dark eyes. The warm August breeze ruffled her cap of dark hair. "I'm thinking . . . I'm thinking!" Actually she was trying to find a good excuse for not helping Mary Harland. But not a single reason popped into her head. Slowly, reluctantly Roxie raised her hand.

The others cheered, and Chelsea said, "It's unanimous!"

"I'm glad," Kathy said in relief. "I already told Mary Roxie would be over to help her."

"Me!" Roxie jumped up, jabbing her finger against her chest. "Me? Why me?"

"Because you're the best artist in the group," Kathy said. "And Mary is a good artist. But if she

she was being, and she smiled and cheered too. She was learning to be like Jesus. He wouldn't make fun of Kathy or scowl at her just because she was entering an art contest.

"Tell me exactly what I have to submit in the contest," Kathy said, settling back in the grass with her knees drawn up to her chin.

"You have to use acrylics and paint a rosebud." Hannah brushed an ant off her bare leg. "It has to be on an 8 x 10 stretched canvas. If you buy the supplies from Zelda Tandee, you get them at a 15 percent discount. Each entry must be submitted by August 20. That's two weeks from now. And that's why we have to help Mary Harland." Hannah looked right at Roxie. "Starting today."

Roxie jumped up. "All right! I'll help her! But I have to ask Mom first."

"She already said you could," Chelsea said with an impish grin.

Roxie started to get angry, then laughed instead. "You had it all figured out, didn't you?"

Chelsea shrugged. "But we had to have a meeting about it, and we had to vote. That's only right."

"Oh, sure." Roxie tugged her pink T-shirt down over her pink shorts. "I'll tell Mom I'm leaving. Or did you girls already do that?"

"We didn't," they all said at once, then giggled.

"See ya later," Roxie called over her shoulder as she ran to the house.

"The meeting is adjourned," Chelsea shouted.

Roxie waved at them and slipped inside the house. The cool air of the air conditioning dried her sweat. Smells of baking cookies drifted from the kitchen along with Mom's voice and Faye's giggles. Roxie ran through the hallway and stopped in the kitchen doorway. Mom was taking chocolate-chip cookies off the cookie sheet, while Faye knelt on a high stool putting lumps of dough on another cookie sheet. Faye was four years old and was eager to learn everything. Her light brown hair was pulled back in two long shiny ponytails and held in place with wide yellow bows. She wore a yellow sunsuit and tiny yellow sandals. Before Roxie could say anything, her sixteen-year-old sister Lacy ran in the back door, jingling the car keys. Her long auburn hair hung almost to her narrow waist. She wore a blue skirt and a print blouse. She worked at Markee's Department Store part-time.

"Mom, I need gas money until I get paid. Could you give me five dollars, please?"

"Look in my purse, Lacy." Mom wiped her hands on a dish towel, then pulled her flowered cotton blouse over her tan shorts. She watched Lacy pull her purse out of the closet and open it. "And try to budget your money better so you don't run out of gas and money at the same time."

"I will, Mom." Lacy waved a five dollar bill.

"Thanks. I'll pay you back tonight." She smiled and ran out the door.

Roxie wrinkled her nose. Lacy usually forgot she even existed. So did Eli. He was fifteen and was always busy working out and eating healthy foods so he could make the football team. Faye was different. She always wanted Roxie to play with her or teach her to read.

Just then Faye spotted Roxie. "Look what I'm doing . . . making cookies with Mom! I even got to dump in the ingredients."

"Good for you." Roxie smiled as she reached for a warm cookie. She liked the gooey hot chocolate chips when she broke the cookie apart. "Mom, is it all right if I go to Mary Harland's house now?"

"Sure." Mom hugged Roxie. "It's really nice of you to want to help her and her family."

Roxie flushed. "See you later." She hurried to the door, then turned back. "Bye, Faye. Keep up the good work."

"I will." Faye dipped in the spoon and lifted out a huge pile of dough.

Eating her cookie, Roxie ran outdoors to her bike. She saw Gracie barking at the neighbor's cat. Gracie belonged to Ezra Menski, the man down the street. Roxie didn't want to think about Ezra right now or to wonder if Grandma Potter had gone out to dinner with him again. Roxie didn't want anyone to think Grandma was going to fall in love with Ezra Menski. That would be terrible!

Roxie shook her finger at Gracie. "Just stay away from our flowers, Gracie." Mom had entered the Prettiest Flowers Contest, and the judging was next week. If they could keep Gracie out of the flowers until then, Mom had a good chance to win. Most of the yards had flowers, but Mom's looked the prettiest.

Several minutes later Roxie leaned her bike against the side of Mary's house and walked around a pile of broken toys and scattered papers to the front steps of the rundown house. Hot wind fluttered the papers and sailed them across the street. A car honked, and a TV blared from inside. Roxie took a deep breath and knocked. The door needed painting. The window beside it was covered with a piece of brown cardboard. A loud crash came from inside the small house. Roxie flinched and knocked again. Why had she agreed to help Mary?

Finally a small girl opened the door, then stood there with her thumb in her mouth, her shirt and shorts wrinkled and dirty and her blonde hair tangled. She was one of Mary's sisters, but Roxie couldn't remember her name.

"Is Mary home?" Roxie looked past the girl into the cluttered living room. Smells of wet diapers turned her stomach.

The little girl studied Roxie, then finally turned, pulled her soggy thumb out of her mouth, and called in a high voice, "Mary, that girl Roxie Shoulders is here to see you."

Roxie chuckled as she stepped into the messy room. The girl reminded her of Faye, except Faye always was clean and her hair always brushed. Two other girls sat on the floor in front of the blaring TV.

Mary rushed from the kitchen, carrying a toddler on her plump hip. Mary's brown hair was cut short and brushed back from her round face. She looked tired and hot. "Roxie! I didn't really think you'd come. I was just feeding Allen."

Allen rubbed a wet, cookie-covered hand across Mary's round cheek. "Cookie."

Mary pulled Allen's hand away. "We'll go to the kitchen." She bent down to her sisters in front of the TV. "Turn that down and scoot back! I won't tell you again!" Her face red, she glanced at Roxie and quickly looked away, then led the way to the small kitchen.

Roxie stopped behind a kitchen chair piled with newspapers. "If this is a bad time, I could come tomorrow."

"It won't be any different. Mom never gets home before 7." Mary plopped Allen in the once-white highchair, pulled down the tray smeared with food, then shoved the newspapers off Roxie's chair.

"Where does your mom work?"

Mary bit her lip. "She doesn't have a job. I don't think she really wants to get one."

"Oh?" Roxie didn't want to hear all of Mary's family secrets, but she didn't know what to say to make her stop talking.

"She likes being free to do what she wants when she wants. I heard her telling Ray—my step-dad—that last night. He doesn't have a job either." Mary's voice was bitter, and she abruptly changed the subject. "It's really nice of you to help me so I can have time to paint the rosebud. I know you're a good artist, and I want to learn all I can from you. I'm going to be a famous artist someday." Mary turned scarlet and shoved a cookie at Allen.

"I'm not that good with acrylics." Roxie slowly sat down. "I'm better at carving things."

"I remember the mouse you did. It was great!"

"Thanks. I just finished a squirrel. It's all right, but I couldn't do it as good as my mom does or as good as my grandpa did before he died."

Mary sighed heavily. "Nobody in my family was ever an artist . . . except maybe my real dad. I don't know anything about him. Mom left him when me and Dan were real little."

Roxie didn't know what to say. She had the same parents she'd always had. So did the other Best Friends. She knew kids whose parents were divorced though.

"Did you see the list of kids who entered?" Mary asked.

Roxie nodded. "It's in the store, and it's not too many. Clay Ross, you, and I have the best chance so far. I know everybody else that's entered."

"I'm not very good at doing flowers."

Roxie knew that. But if she helped Mary, Mary just might win. Impatiently Roxie pushed the thought away. She'd promised to help Mary, and she'd do just that! "I'll help you all I can. Can the girls watch Allen? We could go to your room to work."

Mary shook her head. "The room's too tiny. And it's kind of messy. My three sisters and I share it."

Roxie couldn't imagine such a thing. Her room was huge, and she didn't have to share it with anyone except Faye when she was afraid to sleep alone in her room.

"I can work right here on the table," Mary said.

"Where's your easel and paints?"

Mary cleared her throat. "I don't have an easel, but I do have paints. Would you watch Allen while I get them from the other room? Be sure he doesn't stand up."

Roxie nodded. She smiled at Allen, and he smiled back, showing four tiny white teeth. Wind rattled the small window over the sink stacked with dirty dishes. Water dripped against the bottom of an aluminum pan. Roxie walked to the sink and pushed against the faucet.

"It needs a washer," Mary said stiffly as she walked back in. "My stepdad says he'll fix it, but he never gets to it. My brother Dan would do it, but he doesn't know how." Mary took a deep breath. "Are you sure you want to help me?"

Roxie wasn't sure at all, but she'd agreed to. "I came to help."

Mary sighed in relief and smiled. She washed off Allen's hands and carried him to the front room for the girls to watch.

Roxie flipped open Mary's drawing pad. It was totally filled with drawings, some painted and some not. She knew Mary couldn't afford to waste even a spot of the paper.

Mary walked back in and sank to a chair. "It's hard to get anything done since I have to watch the kids." She jabbed her finger at the roses she'd been sketching. "I can't see what I'm doing wrong."

Roxie remembered the things Mom had showed her a few days ago. "For a rosebud you make a series of overlapping shapes within this basic form." Roxie traced the drawing with the tip of a paintbrush as she talked. "Look how the petals open from the outside as the flower blooms, so that when it's in full bloom it flares out completely from the point where the flower joins the stalk."

"I see! I never saw it before!" Mary's eyes sparkled as she nodded.

"Always pay attention to the direction and pattern of growth to make the flower look real."

"You make it so easy!" Mary leaned toward Roxie. "Someday I want to be rich so I can buy us a house big enough for all of us. I want us to have nice clothes and good food. And I want Dan to be happy. If we had enough money he could quit work when school starts and spend his time studying. He's real smart, and he wants to go to college to study business after high school." Mary flushed again. "You probably don't want to listen to all that, do you?"

Roxie really didn't want to hear it all, but she couldn't very well say that. "I like hearing dreams and plans." She did too—but not Mary's since they weren't really friends.

"I wish dreams could come true," Mary said wistfully.

Roxie remembered what Dad had told her. "Jesus wants to help you, Mary. He'll even help you with your family and your dream to be an artist."

Mary slowly nodded. "I know. I just needed you to remind me. I've been praying. And He sent you to help me!"

Was that true? Roxie walked to the sink, wrinkled her nose at the thought of washing the giant stack, then looked over her shoulder at Mary. "I'll wash the dishes while you work on your rosebud."

2

More Work

Roxie swept the kitchen, then looked over Mary's shoulder as she drew another rose. "You're getting it!"

"I know. Thanks!" Mary's cheeks were flushed as red as a rose. "I can't believe you really and truly are staying to help." She glanced at the round clock on the wall. "Dan should be home soon. He works at Middle Lake Flower Shop. He said he'd bring a real rose home for me to study."

"No kidding! My brother wouldn't think about doing that. My big sister wouldn't either." Roxie put the broom back in the corner with a thoughtful frown. "It must be nice to have a brother who thinks about your work. Eli barely notices my carvings, and then only if Mom or Dad make him look. Lacy's the same way."

"Eli's cute." Mary flushed. "Please *please* don't tell him I said that!"

Roxie laughed. "I won't. I'll go check on the kids." She'd learned the girls were Susan, Jeannie, and Peggy.

Mary's eyes filled with tears. "You'll never know what you did for me today."

Roxie ducked into the other room before she blurted out that she really hadn't wanted to come. Just then Allen tripped over Peggy's doll and sprawled to the floor, crying so loudly he blocked out the blare of the TV. "Don't cry, Allen." Roxie picked him up and cuddled him close. He smelled dirty. She would not change a dirty diaper, not even a disposable one, no matter how nice she was trying to be! Roxie lifted her head and called, "He needs his diaper changed, Mary."

With a laugh Mary took Allen from Roxie. "I thought *you'd* change it."

Roxie grinned. "Sure . . . Any day . . . Right."

Mary pushed her face against Allen as she carried him to her tiny bedroom. She peeled back the tabs and quickly pulled off the wet diaper. "He's got diaper rash real bad, but I don't know what to do about it."

Roxie saw the red sores and quickly turned her head away. "I don't either."

Mary put a clean diaper on Allen and carried the dirty one to the garbage. Struggling against tears, she turned to Roxie. "I think Mom might be thinking of divorcing Ray and kicking him out. I thought she'd be happy once she left Dad and married Ray."

Roxie wanted to cover her ears.

Mary bit her lip. "I guess she was happy for a while, but she's not any more."

Just then Susan tugged on Mary's arm. "I'm hungry."

Jeannie and Peggy ran to Mary. "We're hungry too."

"I'll fix them something." Roxie glanced at the table where Mary had left her paints and things. "You work on your rose. Just tell me what to do."

Mary sat Allen back in the highchair. "I'd better quit working. I can't expect you to do everything for me."

Roxie looked longingly at the door. She did want to leave, but she managed to smile at Mary. "I'll stay a little longer. I could make them a sandwich or something."

Mary smiled in relief. "That's so nice of you! The bread is on that shelf, and the peanut butter is beside it. There's a little jelly left in the refrigerator. You could make them punch to drink, if you want." Mary sent the little girls back to the front room, out of the way. "Roxie will bring your sandwiches to you."

Roxie smeared peanut butter on one slice of bread and jelly on the other, then cut them in fourths. She'd learned to do that for Faye so she wouldn't get so messy. Roxie liked the smell of the peanut butter. She licked her finger and enjoyed the nutty taste. In the front room she had the girls line up on the floor, then gave them each a tiny sandwich and a small glass of punch. Back in the kitchen she broke off bites of a sandwich to feed to Allen. He smeared his face and tray with peanut butter and grape jelly. When they were finished eating she washed all their hands and faces and sat down to read to them. No way would she come again tomorrow! It was too much work, and the house was too messy!

Just then the door opened and Dan walked in. Roxie had seen him in church before, but she'd never paid any attention to him. He was sixteen and had dark hair that went below his collar. His jeans and T-shirt were dirty. He had a rosebud in his hand. He stared at Roxie a long time. "Hi."

Her mouth turned dry. She motioned to the rosebud and smiled. "I see you brought Mary the rose."

He nodded.

Mary stuck her head in. "Dan, you remembered! Thank you!"

He smiled and held it out to her. "I came right home so you could paint."

"Thank you!" Mary held the rose carefully. "Roxie came over to help me so I could work. She did the dishes, swept the floors, and fed the kids!"

Roxie flushed as she slowly stood. "It was nothing."

Dan smiled at Roxie. "Did you enter the contest too?"

She nodded.

"Mary tells me you're good."

Roxie shrugged.

"She's great! She taught me how to draw a rose. Come see what I've done so far." Mary led the way, and Dan followed.

Roxie slowly walked to the kitchen and watched as Dan actually looked at Mary's work and listened to what she said.

Smiling, Dan turned to Roxie. "Thanks . . . for everything."

Roxie's heart melted, and suddenly she was in love. She'd never met a boy like him. She'd be glad to help Mary forever for one smile and a kind word from Dan. She'd come back as often as she could and stay as long as she could! "I guess I'd better get home." She didn't want to leave, but there wasn't any reason to stay with Dan there to help with the kids. She peeled her eyes off Dan and turned to Mary. "See you tomorrow."

"Okay." Mary put her rose in a glass of water. "But you know you don't have to."

"I know." Roxie turned to Dan, and her heart pounded in her chest. He had the most incredible brown eyes! "Bye."

"See you soon, Roxie."

In a daze she told the little girls and Allen good-bye and walked to her bike. The hot wind blew against her as she pedaled down the street. A dog barked at her, but she didn't even hear him. Soon she rode into her yard. Never had the flowers looked more beautiful or the sky so blue or the grass so green . . .

"Roxie . . ." Chelsea called as she ran from her yard into Roxie's.

"Hi." Could Chelsea see the change in her?

"I told the others I'd go help Mary tomorrow so you wouldn't have to."

That brought Roxie back to earth with a thud. She parked her bike in the garage and ran to Chelsea. "I already agreed to help Mary, and I am going to!"

Chelsea shrugged. "Don't get mad."

Roxie flushed. "I'm not mad." But she *was* scared Chelsea would take over the job, and then she'd never get to see Dan except in passing at church. If only she could change ages with Lacy! She got to be in the same Sunday school class with Dan. How lucky!

Chelsea peered closely at Roxie. "Is something wrong?"

"No!" Roxie tried to compose herself. It was too soon to share her wonderful news with anyone, even the Best Friends.

"Guess who I saw today?" Chelsea asked.

Roxie shrugged.

"Clay Ross!" Chelsea sighed and twirled around. Her long red hair flowed out from her slender shoulders. "He was playing tennis at the park. I had to go with Mike." Mike was her eight-year-old brother, and her parents said he was too young to go to the park alone. "Am I ever glad I did!"

For the first time ever Roxie understood how Chelsea felt. "Did he talk to you?"

"No. But he looked at me. I got weak all over and had to sit down." The dreamy look left Chelsea's face. "You won't believe who else was at the park!"

"Who?"

"Your Grandma Potter and Ezra Menski!" Chelsea giggled. "I think they were holding hands."

Roxie's face darkened with anger. "That's not true!"

Chelsea frowned. "I don't lie!"

"Get out of my yard right now! They weren't holding hands, and they never will!"

"Well, don't get mad."

Roxie scowled at Chelsea, then ran to the house and slammed the door after her.

"Is that you, Roxie?" Mom called.

"Yes." Roxie started for the stairs.

"Come to the laundry room, would you?"

"We're doing the washing," Faye shouted.

Slowly Roxie walked to the laundry room. The slosh of the washer and the hum of the dryer were loud. Faye knelt on a chair at the table, folding towels.

Mom looked up as she finished folding a flowered sheet. "How'd it go at Mary's?"

Roxie shrugged. "Okay, I guess. I told her what you told me about drawing a rose."

"Good for you!"

"Will she win the contest instead of you?" Faye asked.

"Maybe."

Mom asked, "Did you meet Mary's mom?"

"She wasn't home. But I met her three sisters and two brothers." A picture of Dan with the rose in his hand flashed across Roxie's mind, and she smiled. She quickly covered it by saying, "I even fixed sandwiches for them. And I did a whole pile of dishes."

"Don't they have a dishwasher?" Faye asked.

Roxie shook her head.

Laughing, Mom hugged Roxie. "As much as you hate doing dishes, you really did do above and beyond the call of duty, didn't you? Will you go back?"

"Tomorrow."

"Can I go and play with the girls?" Faye asked.

"Sorry," Mom said, playfully tugging one of

Faye's ponytails. "You and I are going to the park tomorrow with Grandma."

Roxie locked her fingers together. "Chelsea said Grandma was at the park with Ezra Menski today." Roxie couldn't bring herself to say Chelsea had thought they were holding hands.

"Ezra is a lonely man, Roxie. And Grandma gets lonely too. He and Grandma enjoy being with each other since they're the same age."

Roxie's pink T-shirt and shorts felt too hot. "They better not even think about getting married!"

"Roxie!" Mom frowned and clicked her tongue. "Spending time together is a long way from marriage!"

Faye giggled. "Would that make Ezra Menski our grandpa? And Gracie our dog?"

Mom laughed, but Roxie couldn't. She saw a strained look on Mom's face. Was Mom as upset about the possibility as she was?

They talked a while longer, and then Roxie picked up her bundle of clothes still warm from the dryer and slowly walked down the hall and up the stairs to her room. She dropped her pile of clothes on her bed and sank down beside them. She absently rubbed her hand over her fluffy blue, lavender, and white flowered bedspread. She smelled Lacy's perfume that always hung in the air. What if Grandma Potter did marry Ezra Menski? He was such a grouch! But Hannah liked him, and he liked her.

Roxie bit her lip. He was nicer than he used to be before she'd worked for him. He had called *King's Kids*. The Best Friends as well as several neighborhood kids did odd jobs for pay. Chelsea had organized the business and had named it *King's Kids* because they all belonged to Jesus. Roxie had joined to make extra money. She'd gone to help clean Ezra's kitchen and do his dishes. And on the 4th of July they'd had a surprise birthday party for him. Roxie frowned. That's when she'd first noticed Grandma Potter had a special interest in Ezra.

Roxie jumped up, her fists doubled at her sides. "I don't want to even think about them!" She ran to the basement where her easel was set up so she could work on her painting and stop thinking about Grandma and Ezra.

She ran past the area where Dad had his desk and file cabinet. He had his own construction business. Mom did all kinds of crafts in her own area across the room. She was working on a diorama for Stella Alderman. Roxie peered at the old-fashioned lamppost Mom had carved. Now she was making a man and a woman to stand beside it. Roxie sighed. Would she ever be as good as Mom?

Roxie walked to her easel and studied the rose she was working on. It wasn't nearly as good as Mary's.

What would she do if Dan ever brought *her* a

rose? She wrinkled her nose. Why even daydream about it? He wouldn't do that in a million years.

She stood beside the easel with her hands over her heart and her eyes closed.

"Here's a rose for you," Dan said.

She took the rose and smiled. "Thank you."

"Roxie, are you down there?"

She spun around with a yelp. It wasn't Dan Harland. It was Hannah. "Come on down, Hannah."

"Did you forget about the Best Friends meeting?"

Roxie gasped. "Yes!"

"We're all waiting in Chelsea's yard for you."

Reluctantly Roxie ran up the stairs. Could she face Chelsea after getting angry at her? Roxie followed Hannah outdoors to Chelsea's yard.

Chelsea jumped up, her face red. "I'm sorry for getting mad at you, Roxie."

"Me too." And Roxie meant it. She was glad Chelsea was always quick to apologize.

"Did you remember to bring a Scripture?" Kathy asked.

Roxie dropped her head. They always shared a verse from the Bible. She'd forgotten it was her turn to bring one.

"That's okay." Hannah pulled a paper from the pocket of her shorts. "I have one."

Roxie sat in the shade of the big oak tree in a

circle with Hannah, Kathy, and Chelsea. A bee buzzed around the nearby flowers. Birds sang in the trees.

Hannah rubbed the paper across her knee. "Sometimes I get tired of always helping at home. I found this verse, and I thought it would be good for all of us—especially when we get tired of helping our families or others."

Roxie leaned forward, eager to hear the verse. She had a very hard time helping others, even Mary Harland before Dan came.

"It's Galatians 6:9." Hannah pushed back her straight black hair. "'And let us not be weary in well-doing: for in due season we shall reap, if we faint not.'" Hannah smiled. "If we keep doing good, we'll be rewarded for it."

Roxie thought of the help she was giving Mary. She'd already been rewarded—Dan had talked to her and smiled at her. She opened her mouth to tell the others, then snapped it closed. They might laugh at her just like she laughed at Chelsea for loving Clay Ross.

Roxie held the secret close to her as she thought about tomorrow and Dan.

3

The Red Rose

Roxie stood in the living room doorway and frowned at Faye. "Where did you say Lacy went?"

Faye shrugged so hard her head disappeared between her shoulders.

"She knows I'm supposed to go to Mary Harland's house!" Roxie's voice shot up, and she took a deep breath and forced it back to normal. "She promised to be here to watch you."

Faye pressed into the corner of the couch and stared at Roxie. Her eyes looked big in her small face. "I can watch myself. I'm going to school in September, you know."

"*Preschool*—and you're four, so you can't stay here alone!" Roxie paced the room and stopped at the front window. Today the flowers in the yard looked ugly. She whirled around to Faye. "Where is she?"

Faye twisted her long ponytail around her finger. "Why are you so mad, Roxie?"

Roxie bit her lip. She was afraid she wouldn't get to see Dan today. But she couldn't tell Faye that.

Just then the doorbell rang. Roxie laughed in relief. Maybe it was Chelsea or Hannah. They'd watch Faye until Lacy got home. Roxie flung the door wide, then frowned. No one was there. "Okay, who's playing a stupid trick?" She looked all around but didn't see anyone. She glanced down and gasped in surprise. A single beautiful long-stemmed red rosebud lay on the doorstep with a card hooked to it.

"A flower!" Faye cried.

Roxie gently picked it up. Had Dan brought her a rose? She looked at the card, and her face fell. It was for Lacy!

Faye stared hard at the card. "I love you," she read slowly.

Roxie wanted to fling the rose and the card across the room. Lacy had more boys loving her than any girl she knew.

The back door slammed, and Lacy burst into the room. "Sorry I'm late, girls." She stopped short when she saw the rose. "Is that for me?"

Roxie thrust it at her. "Of course."

Lacy took it and read the card. "But it's not signed!"

"Somebody loves you," Faye said, peering up at the rose and note in Lacy's hand.

Lacy tapped the printed name on the card. "It's from Middle Lake Flower Shop."

Roxie's heart sank. Dan worked there. Would he send Lacy a rose? "I could find out who gave it to you."

"Then do it!" Lacy dropped the card on the end table. "I don't like not knowing who sent it. And I certainly don't want some strange boy loving me. It had better not be from Francis Lisser. He works at the flower shop, and he's always looking at me." Lacy wrinkled her nose. "You find out so I can know if I'm happy or upset."

"I'll find out," Roxie said grimly. It just couldn't be from Dan Harland!

The phone rang, and Lacy grabbed it up. "Hello."

Roxie started to wave good-bye, but the look on Lacy's face stopped her. Lacy frantically motioned for Roxie to come listen. She held the phone so they could both hear.

"Who is this?" Lacy asked sharply.

"Did you get the rose?"

Roxie bit her lip. The voice was low and deep. "Yes."

"Do you like it?"

"Who is this?"

Roxie heard a click and then a dial tone. "Who was it?"

"I don't know!" Lacy tipped back her head and laughed. "It's very romantic."

Faye touched the rose. "Not to me."

"Find out who sent it as soon as you can, Roxie."

"I will. Maybe a neighbor saw who left it." Roxie glanced at her watch. "I have to get over to Mary's. See you later." Maybe Mary would know if Dan would leave a love note and a rose for Lacy. Roxie's stomach knotted. It would be awful if Dan loved Lacy.

Several minutes later Roxie knocked on Mary's door. Susan opened it a crack. She blew a bubble and let it pop.

"Mary's crying and said to go away."

Roxie gently pushed the door wider and slipped inside. The room smelled like strawberry bubble gum. Allen was asleep in his crib, and the other two girls were coloring with books and crayons on the floor. "Where's Mary?"

Susan pointed to the kitchen.

Roxie squared her shoulders and walked around the toys and newspapers into the kitchen. The red rose stood in the middle of the table in a glass of water. Mary sat with her head buried in her arms. Roxie almost turned and ran. But instead she whispered, "I came to help."

Mary lifted her face and brushed at her tears. "Mom says she's getting a divorce from Ray. And he's taking Allen."

Roxie dropped to a chair. This was not what she'd expected to hear. She couldn't think of a thing to say.

"Ray doesn't care a thing about Allen! He won't even see that Allen gets fed."

"Maybe he will."

"And Allen has diaper rash real bad. Ray won't do anything about that."

Roxie locked her hands in her lap. "When's he taking Allen?"

"When he finds a place of his own. He's staying with friends right now, and they won't let him bring the baby."

"So we have time to think of something."

Mary's face brightened. "Will you help me?"

Roxie's heart sank. What was she getting herself into? "I said I would, didn't I?"

Mary took a deep, shuddering breath. "I prayed for help. I said if none came today, I'd take Allen and run away."

"You won't really run away, will you?"

Mary shook her head. "Not since you came."

Roxie sank low in her chair. She was here to help Mary only because of Dan. What would happen if Mary learned the truth? "Did you do more work on your painting?"

"Some." Mary showed her drawings to Roxie. "I'm getting better, thanks to you."

Roxie studied the flowers. They were as good as Mom could've done. Roxie's heart sank. Was it possible Mary would indeed win the contest?

"Well?"

Roxie managed to smile. "This one is especially good."

"That's what I told her."

Roxie whirled around to find Dan right behind her. He wore a light blue T-shirt and faded jeans. Her pulse leaped, and chills ran up and down her spine. "Hi."

"I didn't hear you come in," Mary said.

Dan grinned. "I was quiet. I knew it was Allen's nap time."

Every word Roxie had ever learned vanished from her tongue and mind.

"I don't have to be back to work for two hours, so I came to take the kids to the park." Dan smiled at Roxie. "Want to come?"

She nodded hard.

Mary sighed. "I wish I could go, but I'll paint while you're gone." She hugged Roxie close. "Thanks. You're a good friend."

Roxie flushed to the roots of her hair. Silently she followed Dan to the front room to get the girls. He kept them quiet as he walked them outdoors.

"Now you can shout for glee, girls," he said with a laugh.

Susan jumped up and down, clapped, and shouted. Jeannie and Peggy ran around in circles, shouting as loudly as they could. Finally they ran down the sidewalk ahead of Dan and Roxie.

Dan glanced at Roxie. "I noticed Mary had been crying. I suppose she told you about Mom and Ray."

"She did. She's afraid Ray will take Allen."

"He will. Mary's really upset."

"Aren't you?"

"I figure it'll be one less for her to take care of."

"She doesn't see it that way." Roxie walked around a toy truck on the sidewalk. "I told her I'd help her find a way to keep him."

"I don't know what you can do, but thanks." Dan smiled.

The smile zoomed to Roxie's heart and stayed there all the way to the park.

"There's Lacy," Dan said, pointing toward the swings. "And your little sister."

Roxie nodded. Had Dan's voice changed when he said Lacy's name? Was he looking at her like he longed to be at her side? Roxie had seen that look often on boys' faces when Lacy was around.

"Can we play with Faye?" Susan asked, tugging on Dan's hand.

"Sure." Dan ran with them to the swings.

Roxie followed slowly as Dan and Lacy exchanged greetings. Dan had totally forgotten about her. As soon as he had seen Lacy, it was as if she didn't exist.

Faye twisted the swing and smiled at Roxie. "Push me, Roxie!"

She pushed Faye and then the other girls while Dan and Lacy talked and laughed. Tears burned the backs of Roxie's eyes, but she wouldn't let them fall. Had Dan sent the rose to Lacy? Roxie thought of the voice on the phone and listened to Dan. She couldn't tell if he'd been the one who'd called.

As soon as she could Roxie said, "I'm going home. Tell Mary I'll see her another day."

"Sure. Bye." Dan waved at Roxie and turned back to Lacy.

"See you at home," Lacy said.

Roxie nodded. She couldn't speak without bursting into tears. Slowly she walked away, her head down.

"Roxie!" Dan called.

She spun around. He wanted her to stay!

"You left your bike at our house."

Her heart sank. She nodded.

"If you want, I'll ride it to work and bring it to you afterward."

"That's fine." Roxie spun around and raced across the park away from Dan and Lacy. Just as Roxie reached the edge of the park she saw

Grandma Potter and Ezra Menski walking side by side, deep in conversation. They didn't notice her. She looked carefully to see if they were holding hands. They weren't, and she felt a little better. She didn't want to talk to them or anyone else right now. She ducked behind a tree and waited until they stopped at the wishing well with their backs to her.

She ran all the way home and burst into the house, her face wet with sweat and her chest heaving. She dropped to the front room floor and let the air conditioner cool her off. Her head whirled. How was she going to get Lacy to ignore Dan?

An idea popped into Roxie's head, and she sat up with a cry. She'd find out who sent Lacy the rose and wrote her the love note! If it was someone besides Dan, Lacy would fall madly in love with him and forget all about Dan Harland!

Roxie raced upstairs to Lacy's room and picked up the note beside the vase that held the rosebud. She studied the note. It was printed and not hand-written, so it would be hard to learn who'd done it. She pushed the card into the pocket of her shorts and ran back downstairs. "I'm going to play detective." She grinned. "Where are my dark glasses?"

She slipped outdoors. Hannah loved to solve mysteries. "I'll see if she'll go with me."

Roxie ran across the street to Hannah's yard, past the huge rock that stood near the sidewalk, and right up to the door. Roxie pushed the doorbell, and

Hannah answered it almost immediately. The smell of grilled cheese sandwiches hung in the air. "Want to help me solve a mystery, Hannah?"

"Sure!" Hannah's black eyes flashed with excitement. "Let me tell Mom I'm going with you."

Roxie fingered the card as Hannah dashed to the kitchen to tell her mom. In a minute she was back, asking about the details. Roxie told her about the rose and showed her the card as they walked toward the flower shop three blocks away.

"What'll you say when we get there?"

Roxie shrugged. "I don't know."

A few minutes later she stopped on the sidewalk outside the flower shop and looked up the wide steps to the big door decorated with bows and a grapevine wreath. "Here goes. If you spot anyone who looks suspicious, let me know."

"I will."

Roxie opened the heavy door. The bell tinkled. The room smelled of flowers and potting soil and potpourri. Flowers stood in vases of different sizes inside a huge refrigerated display case. Shelves were lined with plants of all kinds. Another shelf held vases of different sizes and prices. No one was in the room.

"Now what?" Hannah whispered.

Roxie took a deep breath. "Hello. Anybody here?" Mom always did that, and it had always embarrassed Roxie, but she didn't know what else to do.

A teenage boy stuck his head out the door that led to the back room where the flower arrangements were put together and boxed. He wore a brown apron over his T-shirt and jeans. He was short with a thin face and dark hair all the way to his collar. "Hi, girls. Can I help you?"

"Aren't you Francis Lisser?" Hannah asked.

"Yes."

Roxie bit back a cry. This was the very boy Lacy didn't like! Roxie stepped forward. "Someone sent my sister a single red rosebud from here yesterday."

Hannah pointed to the desk where the cash register sat with papers scattered around it and others stuck on a spindle. "Would there be a record of it? Lacy Shoulders at The Ravines . . . 2960 Ash Street."

Francis cleared his throat. "I'll check." He flipped through the papers. "Are you sure it was from this flower shop?"

Hannah nodded.

Roxie listened to his voice to see if it was the same as on the phone. She couldn't tell. She looked at the display of cards on the desk and found a copy like the one in her pocket. Nobody would buy a rose somewhere else and get the card from here.

"Nothing here." Francis spread his hands wide. "Sorry."

"Thanks anyway." Roxie walked across to the refrigerated display case and studied the vase of long-stemmed red roses. Maybe Francis had taken the rose from here without filling out a receipt for it.

"Tell Lacy hello for me," Francis said with a hesitant smile.

Hannah nodded. "We will."

Roxie looked around again and walked out with Hannah close behind her. The bell tinkled on the door. Roxie squinted in the bright sunlight. "Did he look guilty?"

"I couldn't tell."

Roxie looked up and down the street. A car dealership was on one side of the street and a filling station on another. Was it time for Dan to come back to work yet? Did he know who had sent the rose? Roxie bit her lip. Had *he*? She had to know.

Hannah touched Roxie's arm. "You look ready to cry. What's wrong?"

Roxie rubbed her hand down her shorts. The words were on the end of her tongue, but she wouldn't let them spill out. Hannah would never understand about Dan and her and Lacy. She didn't understand it herself. "Let's go home."

"What's the next step?"

Roxie shook her head. "I have no idea."

"We could stake out the place."

"Watch it, you mean?"

"Yes!" Hannah giggled. "We could stay out of sight in that car lot and see who comes out with a single red rose."

"It sounds pretty boring."

"Don't you want to try?"

Roxie frowned in thought. "All right . . . But not today."

"How come?"

"I'm too hot and tired." Roxie forced back the lump in her throat. She was actually too sad when she thought about Dan forgetting all about her just to talk to Lacy at the park, but she couldn't say that. She sighed from deep inside. "Let's go home."

4

Another Red Rose

Roxie leaned against the tree in her yard and held the book so it looked like she was reading it. She'd grabbed the first book she'd found. It was one Dad had been reading on building decks and porches. Hopefully nobody would notice. She looked over the top of the book and looked around. Dan would be out of work by now and would be on his way with her bike. She wanted to see him without Lacy being around.

Gracie stopped at the edge of the yard and barked.

Roxie jumped up and shook her book at Gracie. "Get home!" Gracie turned and ran. Roxie sank back to the grass. She watched an ant carrying something large and white to its hill of sand. Across the street Hannah's three sisters shouted and played. Hannah had taken her baby brother for a walk in his stroller. Roxie leaned back against the tree.

Would Hannah tease her about loving Dan Harland if she knew about it?

She heard the crunch of tires on the pavement, and her heart stood still. Slowly she turned her head. Dan was wheeling into the driveway. He'd changed into a black T-shirt, and his hair was combed neatly. He looked toward the house. Was he wishing Lacy would come out?

Roxie jumped up and hid the book behind her back. "Hi, Dan."

"Hi, Roxie. I didn't see you." Dan looked down at the bike. "Is there a special place you want this?"

She ran to him and showed him where to park it beside the other bikes. "Thanks for bringing it back."

"No problem."

"I didn't know you knew where we lived."

"I sometimes go home this way." He noticed the book in her hand. "What're you reading?"

She flushed scarlet. "Nothing much."

He took it from her and looked at the picture of decks on the cover. "I didn't know you were interested in building. That's great."

She took the book and stuck it behind her back. "Are you ready for school to start?"

"I guess."

"Will you be a junior?"

He nodded. "So will Lacy."

"Right."

"Is she home?"

"Yes. She's probably talking to some boy on the phone." Roxie saw the pain cross Dan's face. "She's always talking to some boy."

"Oh." Dan bit his lip. "Well, I guess I'll head on home."

"You might as well."

"Maybe I'll see you tomorrow."

Roxie's pulse fluttered. "Sure. What time do you get off work?"

"Three." Dan looked toward the house again, then loped away.

Roxie watched until he was out of sight.

The next day Roxie left Mary's early after helping her with the housework and the kids. She pedaled home so she was there by 3. She had a funny feeling Dan would go home this way in hopes of seeing Lacy. "Why can't he just forget about her?"

Her stomach in knots, Roxie hid behind a bush and waited. She rubbed her icy hands down her jeans. She wasn't really cut out to be a spy. But she simply had to know if Dan had brought the rose to Lacy. Sometimes she was positive he hadn't; other times she was afraid he had.

Just then Grandma Potter and Ezra Menski walked into the yard. Dressed in light blue slacks and a blue and white blouse, Grandma was short and slender with white hair combed back from her oval face. She looked flushed and happy. Ezra leaned slightly on his cane. His gray trousers hung on his bony frame. He wore a hat that covered his balding white head. They stopped near the bush where Roxie hid. She held her breath and forced back a groan.

Ezra caught Grandma's hand and held it to his heart. "Emma, why can't we talk about marriage? We care about each other very much."

Roxie wanted to leap out and scream at the top of her lungs, but she stayed hidden. Grandma would scold her for eavesdropping if she showed herself now.

"Ezra, my family's not ready for that yet. Give them more time . . . Please."

"I'm over seventy, Emma. I don't want to give them more time."

Roxie bit her lip hard enough to taste blood. How she hated Ezra Menski! How dare he want to marry Grandma!

Smiling, Grandma patted Ezra's arm. "Ilene's waiting for us. Let's go have coffee with her and talk about this later."

Roxie wanted to shout, "Don't ever talk about it!," but she kept silent. She watched them walk to the front door and ring the doorbell. Faye opened the door for them, greeted them cheerfully, and invited them in. Roxie groaned and blinked back tears. What would Grandpa Potter say if he knew

Grandma wanted to get married again? Grandpa lived in Heaven, but he still might feel bad about it.

Roxie moved restlessly. Maybe she should quit watching for Dan and go inside to make sure Ezra didn't say a word about marriage. Dan might not even walk home this way. Just as she decided to quit spying she heard someone coming. She peeked around the bush, and her heart almost stopped. Dan was walking toward the front door with a long green flower box under his arm. He looked nervous. He stopped and looked toward the front door, then looked all around. Roxie sank lower behind the bush. Could he see her?

Taking a deep breath, Dan ran lightly to the door and set the green box against the door. He pressed the doorbell and raced to a nearby bush and ducked behind it.

Roxie pressed her hands to her spinning head. Dan had left the rose for Lacy!

The door opened, and Faye stood there. She looked all around but didn't look down. She slammed the door closed without seeing the flower box.

Dan slowly stood. He hiked up his jeans and twisted the toe of his sneaker in the grass. Frowning, he looked toward the house and toward the street. Finally he ran away.

Roxie leaped to the front door and snatched up the box. She darted back around the bush and dropped to the ground. Her breathing sounded loud enough for the entire neighborhood to hear. She fanned her face with her hand and tried to slow the rapid beat of her heart. Trembling, she pulled the white ribbon off the box and lifted the lid. She folded back the white paper. It crackled. A long-stemmed red rosebud was nestled inside on a frilly green fern. She rubbed an unsteady hand over her dry mouth, then lifted out the small white card. "Lacy, I'd like to give you a dozen, but one will have to do. With all my love." It wasn't signed. Roxie flung the card inside the box and rammed the lid back on. "I hate him!"

Tears glistened in her eyes. She knew she didn't really hate him. She just wanted him to love her like she loved him.

A few minutes later Roxie crept into the house and upstairs. She heard Lacy in her room. Should she keep the rose from her? Roxie shook her head. Her cheeks pink and her eyes snapping, she stepped into Lacy's room and thrust the box at her. "Here!"

Lacy laughed breathlessly. "Another rose for me? I wonder who sent it."

"Dan Harland!"

Lacy frowned, and her hands grew quiet on the box. "How do you know?"

"I saw him leave it at the door!"

"But he works at the flower shop. Maybe he only delivered it."

Roxie grasped at the tiny straw of hope. "Do you think so?"

"Of course! Dan wouldn't leave flowers at the door and run away. He's not that shy."

"Are you sure?" Oh, let it be true!

"I think he probably delivered the rose for someone else."

Roxie laughed and nodded, suddenly eager to believe Lacy. "I'll find out!"

"Good." Lacy carefully slipped the rose and the fern into the vase with the other rose that was open slightly. The aroma drifted across the room. They looked beautiful sitting on the white lace doily in the middle of Lacy's desk. Lacy touched the new rose with her fingertip. "Oh, but they're beautiful!" She turned to Roxie. "This is so romantic! I hope I like the boy who's sending them." Her face hardened. "And it had better not be Francis Lisser!"

Suddenly Roxie hoped it was. Better Francis than Dan!

Lacy clipped her long auburn hair back with two wide red barrettes. "I've got to get to work. Let me know when you solve the red rose mystery." Lacy laughed as she slipped on her flat red shoes.

Roxie slowly walked to her room and sank down on her desk chair. How could she learn who'd given Lacy the roses? Roxie fingered her *I'm A Best Friend* button. Should she talk to Hannah again and get her help? Maybe if all four of them worked together, they could solve the mystery. The tiny stubborn fear that Dan had indeed given Lacy the roses stopped Roxie from calling the Best Friends.

A few minutes later Roxie heard Lacy run down the stairs and call good-bye to the others. The front door slammed just as the phone rang. Roxie jumped. She raced to answer the phone in the hall near Lacy's room. "Hello," Roxie said in a low, breathless voice.

"Do you like the rosebud, Lacy?"

Roxie swallowed hard. "Yes." He thought she was Lacy! Was it Dan? She couldn't tell. "Who are you?"

"A special friend."

"Tell me your name or I'll hang up!"

"No! Wait."

"Tell me!"

"Did the notes make you mad?"

Roxie licked her dry lips. "No."

"I wish I had the courage to give them to you in person."

Suddenly Roxie recognized the voice. It was Dan! She sagged against the wall, her face damp with perspiration. "Dan Harland, I know it's you!"

"I'm sorry, Lacy. I was afraid I didn't stand a chance with you."

What could she say to stop him from loving Lacy? Before she knew the words were there, they popped out of her mouth. "I wouldn't go out with you if you were the last boy alive!"

Roxie slammed down the receiver and clamped her hand over her mouth. How could she be so cruel? Had he recognized her voice there at the end?

She ran to her room, closed the door, and leaned against it, her chest rising and falling.

Dan loved Lacy!

Roxie burst into tears and flung herself across the bed. After a long time she sat up, blew her nose, and wiped her eyes dry with a soft tissue. Lacy didn't know Dan had sent the roses. Roxie pressed the tissue into a ball. "What if I just don't tell her?" she whispered. Lacy would never know and so would never go out of her way to talk to Dan. Dan would be too heartbroken to speak to Lacy again.

Roxie paced her room as wild thoughts spun around inside her head. She dropped the wadded tissue into the wastebasket. She saw her Bible on her desk and looked quickly away. She sure wasn't being like Jesus.

She lifted her chin. "I don't care!" But deep inside she did care. She felt fresh tears start, and she dashed them away.

She crept downstairs. She smelled coffee and heard voices from the kitchen. She eased open the basement door and tiptoed down the stairs. Maybe working on her project would help. She picked up a pad of paper and drew a quick sketch of a rose. It looked ugly. She looked at the old canvas she'd been practicing on. "Faye could do a better job," she muttered angrily. She tried to draw the layout of the rosebud and the vase, but nothing came out right.

Impatiently she turned away from her drawing and picked up the little squirrel she'd carved. She'd used Grandpa Potter's special carving tools to do the finishing touches on the squirrel. She turned it over and over in her hands. "It's ugly!" She set it back on the shelf beside the special tools and turned her back on all her projects.

"I have no talent! Nobody loves me!" She whimpered and covered her face with her cold hands. "*I* am ugly!"

5

The Best Friends

With an angry flick of her brush Roxie painted a red X across the ugly rose she'd just finished. "I might as well give up and watch cartoons with Faye! I'll never paint again." Roxie flopped down on her bed. This morning she'd brought the paints and easel to her room so she could work without Dad or Mom talking to her. Saturday mornings they usually worked in the basement at their desks. They were probably still in the kitchen, laughing and talking over their Saturday morning waffles. Dad liked waffles. He said they tasted best on Saturday morning when he could take as long as he wanted to eat them.

Roxie wrinkled her nose. She would've eaten a waffle too, but this morning she could manage only a banana and a glass of cold milk. Faye was probably still wearing the sticker off the banana on her

58

forehead. Roxie rolled her eyes. Sometimes Faye was such a baby!

Roxie punched her pillow. "I wish I was a baby instead of twelve!"

Someone knocked on her door, and she jumped up. "Leave me alone, Faye! I told you I wouldn't read to you."

"It's me, Roxie."

"And me."

"Me too."

Roxie heard the Best Friends, and she froze in place. She wasn't in the mood to listen to them or even to see them. She'd stayed away from them for three days—ever since she'd learned Dan had given roses to Lacy. "I'm busy," Roxie called, forcing her voice to sound cheerful.

"We know something's wrong," Chelsea said. She rattled the knob. "Open up."

"We're not going away," Kathy said, and Hannah agreed.

Her stomach a tight ball of ice, Roxie stepped to the door. "You won't want to talk to me today. I'm in a terrible mood."

"We do want to talk."

"We're not leaving!"

With a ragged sigh Roxie unlocked the door and slowly opened it. The smell of waffles and coffee drifted around the Best Friends. Roxie nervously rubbed her hand down her wrinkled blouse and old blue shorts. The Best Friends looked fresh and bright and were dressed in neat, clean shorts and T-shirts. They all wore their *I'm A Best Friend* buttons. Without a word she opened the door wider, waited until they stepped in, then closed and locked it. The smell of waffles and coffee stayed in the hallway.

Chelsea dropped to the carpet with her back against the bed. "We came to help."

"We did." Hannah and Kathy sat with Chelsea.

Roxie tugged at her wrinkled blouse and scowled at her unmade bed. Finally she sank cross-legged to the floor and sat on her hands. She hadn't bothered brushing her hair, and she could feel pieces of it sticking in the air. Impatiently she combed it with her fingers and rubbed it flat, then sat on her hands again.

"Paul and Sonya Crandall came home day before yesterday." Chelsea folded her arms and looked smug. "They said we did a very good job taking care of their place while they were gone so long. They said they'd find homes for the kittens now that they're old enough and that if any of us wants one, we can have it."

Roxie shook her head. "I can't have one." Right now she didn't want one. She only wanted to be left alone.

"And Betina Quinn called me," Kathy said. "She's taking Mark and Allie for a long trip before school starts. And when they come back, she and Lee Malcomb are getting engaged."

"Isn't that great?" Hannah asked.

Roxie couldn't get excited, but she managed to say, "Great."

"We all have jobs for next week." Chelsea smiled proudly.

Roxie reluctantly listened to the rest of the news. She had missed out on a lot by not talking to them for three days!

Hannah flipped back her long, black hair. The smell of apple shampoo drifted out from it. "Now tell us what's new with Mary Harland."

Roxie flushed. "I don't know."

"You don't?"

Roxie looked down at her bare knees. There was a spot of red paint on one of them. "I haven't seen her for three days."

The girls were quiet a long time. Finally Chelsea said, "This is worse than we thought."

"What's wrong, Roxie?" Kathy asked.

Hannah added, "Did something terrible happen that you're afraid to tell us about?"

Roxie sniffed and rubbed a hand over her eyes. She could smell the grape gum Kathy was chewing. "I don't want to say."

"But you must!" Chelsea leaned forward eagerly. "It's why we came!"

"Tell us," Hannah and Kathy said together. They looked at each other and grinned.

Roxie took a deep breath. She could tell the girls really wanted to know what was bothering her. "I can't . . . can't paint . . . or draw . . . or carve."

"But why not?" Kathy cried.

Roxie shook her head slightly.

Hannah leaned forward, her black eyes wide. "You have so much talent!"

"Not any more." Absently Roxie scratched at the blob of red paint on her knee. The warm breeze ruffled her curtains and brought in the smell of freshly mowed grass.

Chelsea touched Roxie's hand. "Tell us what happened to you."

Roxie waved at her canvas. "Look! I tried to paint a rose and I couldn't. I can't even finish in time for the contest deadline!"

"We knew something was wrong." Kathy studied Roxie thoughtfully. "That's why we're here."

Roxie bit her bottom lip. "I can't talk about it."

"Yes, you can!" Chelsea cried.

"We're your best friends," Kathy said gently.

"You can talk to us," Hannah whispered.

Roxie glanced at the Best Friends, and giant tears welled up in her eyes. Slowly she shook her head. "It'll make you all hate me."

"Never!"

"Tell us anyway!"

"I . . . aah . . . haven't been to help Mary Harland in three . . . days."

"How come?" Kathy asked.

Hannah took a deep breath. "Do you think she might win the contest if you keep helping her?"

Roxie shrugged. How could she tell them about Dan and her broken heart and the mean thing she'd done?

"We know you have a very good reason for hiding away for three days, Roxie. Now tell us!" Chelsea sounded firm.

"We won't be mad," Kathy said.

Roxie pressed her hands to her hot cheeks. "I know I should help her like I promised. But why can't one of you do it instead of me?"

"Tell us what's wrong!" Chelsea cried.

Suddenly a dam seemed to burst inside Roxie, and she told them about loving Dan and helping Mary because of it and Dan bringing roses for Lacy and the phone conversation between her and Dan with him thinking it was Lacy. Roxie threw up her hands. "I am ugly and rotten and worse than the worst person in the whole entire world!" She ducked her head and wrapped her arms around it.

"We love you, Roxie," Hannah said softly.

Kathy patted Roxie's arm. "So does Jesus."

Chelsea sighed heavily. "Now you know how it feels to love a boy who doesn't love you back."

Roxie sniffed and slowly lowered her arms and

lifted her head. Tears sparkled in her dark eyes. "I don't know what to do."

Kathy squeezed Roxie's hand. "Yes, you do! Ask Jesus to forgive you and then get back to helping Mary."

"And tell Lacy about Dan," Hannah said.

Chelsea gasped. "Tell Lacy? But she loves Dan!"

Roxie chewed on her bottom lip.

"Christians tell the truth," Kathy said firmly. "We all know that. Right?"

"Right!" Hannah nodded.

"Right," Chelsea whispered, her face as red as her hair.

Roxie nodded. "I'll tell her, but it won't be easy."

"Our Heavenly Father will help you," Kathy said.

"That's right," Chelsea agreed.

"We can pray right now," Hannah suggested quietly.

Roxie blinked back fresh tears as she bowed her head. How could she even pray? She was too bad!

"Jesus said to forgive." Kathy took a deep breath. "That means forgiving yourself too, Roxie."

Roxie barely nodded. "Jesus, I'm sorry for doing the wrong I did. Please forgive me. And help me to forgive myself."

"Heavenly Father, thank You for all the help you always give us," Hannah prayed softly. "You're good to us all the time. We want to do what You want us to do. Show us how to help Roxie and Mary and Dan and even Lacy. In Jesus' name, Amen."

A great weight lifted off Roxie, and she smiled at the Best Friends, her first smile in three long days. "Thank you for coming."

"Sure," they all said together, then giggled.

"I guess this means I'd better go help Mary." Roxie pushed herself up. "I don't know what she'll say since I've been gone this long. And I told her I'd see what to do about Allen's diaper rash."

"My mom has some special stuff for it," Hannah said. "I'll get it from her, and you can take it to Mary."

"I wish it was that easy to help her mom get a job."

"We could tell our parents, and maybe they could help," Kathy said. "Find out what she can do and tell us."

"It's too bad she's too old to work with the *King's Kids*." Chelsea grinned, then frowned. "I still don't have my phone bill paid! It takes a long, long time to earn three hundred dollars!" Chelsea had called her best friend in Oklahoma after she'd moved to Michigan and had talked to her a long time each day. She was still paying the bill.

Kathy leaped up, her eyes sparkling. "I have a great idea! Chel, when you get calls for us to do odd jobs, ask the person who calls if they need somebody full-time! We can tell Mrs. Harland about any job that might be open."

"But don't do it until we learn just what Mrs. Harland can do," Roxie said. She hoped Mary would like their idea. It sounded like it would work.

Hannah glanced at Roxie's bedside clock. "Oh no, it's almost noon, and I told Mom I'd make lunch for the girls! Roxie, stop over and get the stuff for diaper rash when you're ready." Hannah dashed out the door, calling good-bye over her shoulder.

Kathy walked toward the door. "I have to get home too. I'm glad you told us what was bothering you."

Roxie smiled. "Thanks for coming."

"See ya later!" Kathy hurried away, leaving the door open behind her.

Roxie slowly brushed her hair while she checked in her closet to see what she should wear. What would she do if she saw Dan today? Shivers ran up and down her back.

"It's really really hard to be in love." Chelsea sighed heavily and leaned against the door frame.

"Especially when he doesn't love you back." Roxie choked on the last few words. She hadn't said them aloud before.

Chelsea lifted her chin and squared her shoulders. "I will find a way to make Clay love me!"

"Forget it, Chel. He won't."

Chelsea's eyes flashed. "Oh yes, he will! I'll find a way. Wait and see!" She flipped back her hair, walked out of the room, and ran down the stairs.

Roxie quickly changed into a new yellow T-shirt with two teddy bears on it and a pair of blue shorts. What would she say to Dan if she saw him today? She groaned from deep inside.

A few minutes later she picked up the salve from Hannah's mom and rode her bike along the busy street to Mary's house. The smell of exhaust fumes filled the air. Three boys on skateboards zipped along the sidewalk, their wheels loud on the concrete. A black squirrel ran up the side of a tree and hid among the leaves.

Roxie clutched her handlebars and stared at Mary's front door. Her heart hammered so hard, the bears on her T-shirt danced. Would Dan be home?

6

More Help for Mary

Roxie hesitated, then knocked on the Harlands' door. She wanted to leap on her bike and ride away. The wind blew papers against the curb across the street. A car drove past with music blaring from it.

Susan opened the door but didn't speak or smile. She wore a dirty T-shirt and shorts too big for her small body.

"Is Mary home?"

"Yes."

"Tell her I'm here, will you?"

Susan stepped aside. The other two girls were watching a cartoon on TV. They glanced at Roxie, then turned back to the cartoon.

Roxie stepped over a doll as she headed for the kitchen. The room was hot and smelled closed-in and dirty. "Is Mary in the kitchen?"

Susan pointed toward the bedroom.

Roxie hesitated, then walked to the bedroom

and opened the door. Mary lay on the bed dressed
in baggy shorts and shirt. She was sobbing hard with
Allen sound asleep beside her. The tiny room was
almost filled with the double bed that was pushed
tight against the wall. Boxes stood side by side
against a wall inside the doorless closet. It was obvi-
ous the girls used the boxes as a dresser. A few
dresses hung there along with jeans and blouses.
Roxie started to back out the door, but she remembered how good it had felt for the Best Friends to
help her. Mary needed even more help than she had
needed.

"Mary . . . Mary, it's Roxie."

Mary gasped and turned a tear-wet face to
Roxie. "I didn't know you were here."

"Susan let me in. I came to help you."

Mary flushed scarlet as she rubbed her face dry.
"I didn't want you to see me cry."

"I brought salve for Allen's diaper rash.
Hannah's mom says it works fast."

"Thanks." Mary stuck it on the closet shelf.
"I'll rub it on him when he wakes up."

"What can I do to help?"

Mary plucked at her loose-fitting blouse.
"Nothing. I'm not going to finish the painting."

"But why not?"

"I can't."

"I'll take care of the kids and do your dishes."

Allen whimpered and flipped over. Mary

spread a light blanket over him and turned back to Roxie in the doorway. "If you really want to help me, find a place for me and Allen to live."

"But you live here!"

Mary shook her head hard. "Not for long. Let's talk in the kitchen so Allen can sleep. He didn't get much sleep last night."

Roxie saw the dark circles under Mary's eyes. "Were you up with him all night?"

"Mom was too tired to get up." Mary led the way to the cluttered kitchen.

Roxie smelled peanut butter from the open jar on the table. Water dripped in the sink. A grocery bag beside the back door was full of trash. Feeling helpless, Roxie sat at the table across from Mary. "Now, tell me what in the world you were talking about—what do you mean, a place for you and Allen?"

Mary chewed on her lip as she screwed the lid onto the peanut butter jar. "Ray and Mom are getting a divorce. Mom says she's going to find a job, but she goes to visit her friends instead. Ray says he's taking Allen." Mary's chin trembled, and she locked her hands together on the table. "I can't let him do that! I've taken care of Allen ever since he was born. He needs me."

Roxie's heart turned over. This was a problem she couldn't solve. "I don't know what to say."

"Do you know where I could go with Allen?"

Roxie shook her head. "I'll talk to my mom. She'll know what to do. Just don't run away before I can get help for you."

Mary was quiet a long time. "Okay, I won't. Ray won't find a place for a while. He's so lazy! That gives me more time."

Roxie knew she wanted to tell Mary God would help her, but it wasn't as easy for her to say it as was for Hannah or Kathy. They grew up talking that way. Finally Roxie blurted out, "Mary, you know God answers prayer, don't you?"

"Yes."

"We'll pray for the right answer. And it sure can't be you running away with Allen. You're too young to live on your own."

"I know," Mary whispered. "But that's all I could think of. I didn't know what to do. And you didn't come for three days."

Roxie's ears and neck burned with shame. "I'm sorry. But I'm here now. So, get out your paints and get to work."

Mary's face lit up. "Are you sure?"

"Positive!"

Mary hurried to get her things while Roxie cleaned off the table. Mary spread out her work as she showed Roxie several rosebuds she'd painted.

"You're doing better all the time," Roxie said in admiration.

The girls in the front room screamed, and

Roxie ran to settle the problem. Jeannie and Peggy wanted the same doll, and Susan was trying to keep them quiet so she could watch TV. Roxie picked up a book. "Want to hear a story? I'll read it to you."

Susan clicked off the TV. "I like that story."

Roxie sat on the lumpy sofa with Jeannie on her lap, Peggy on one side, and Susan on the other. The book cover looked like Allen had chewed on it. Faye had the very same book, but hers was in perfect shape and still looked brand-new. Roxie read the story just like she'd read it to Faye. She read two other books too, and the girls wanted still another one. But Allen cried, and Roxie hurried to get him.

She picked him up and wrinkled her nose at the smell. She turned to Susan. "Tell Mary Allen needs changing, will you?"

Susan nodded, turned, and shouted, "Mary, Allen needs his diaper changed and Roxie Shoulders won't do it!"

Roxie laughed and handed him over to Mary. "Mrs. Shigwam said to wash him first with warm, soapy water, then rinse him with warm, clean water. After that, rub the salve on kind of thick."

Mary followed the directions exactly while Allen cried at the top of his lungs. She hugged him close and patted his back until he finally stopped sobbing. She set him in his highchair and held a glass of milk for him to drink, then gave him a cracker.

"He's sure cute." Roxie smiled. Had Dan

looked like Allen when he was a baby? Roxie's heart jerked. She dare not think about Dan!

While Mary worked on her art again, Roxie pulled coloring books and crayons out from the top shelf of the closet near the front door. The little girls laid on their stomachs on the floor and colored quietly. Roxie picked up the toys and papers off the floor and made the room as tidy as she could. There were just too many people and not enough space! Her house was big enough to share with the Harlands, but she knew that was impossible.

Just then the door opened, and Dan stepped inside. Roxie's heart zoomed to her feet. Dan looked tired and sad.

"Hi." Dan smiled slightly.

"Hi." Roxie's voice broke, and she swallowed hard.

"Is Mary in the kitchen?"

Roxie nodded. She couldn't speak around the giant lump in her throat.

Dan walked to the kitchen, and Roxie slowly followed.

"Dan!" Mary's eyes widened in surprise. "How come you're home in the middle of the day? Are you sick?"

He shook his head. "I asked if I could take off early." He turned to Roxie. "I can watch the kids now if you want to go home."

Tears burned the backs of her eyes. Was he sad

because of what she'd done to him? She shrugged.
"I can stay a little longer."

"It's up to you." Dan peered over Mary's shoulder and studied her work. "It looks good." He glanced up. "Don't you think so, Roxie?"

She nodded. Oh, why couldn't she talk to him?

"I like this leaf." Dan pointed to a leaf Mary had just painted.

"I like it too," Mary said.

"It's nice," Roxie whispered. She flushed painfully. Maybe she *should* leave.

Dan lifted Allen from the highchair. "I'll take the kids to the park for an hour so you can work, Mary. Want to come, Roxie?"

Her pulse tingled, and her legs turned to quickset Jello. She nodded.

Mary laughed and flung out her arms. "I can't believe I'll have a whole hour of silence while I work! I'll probably be so excited I won't be able to do anything."

Roxie forced a laugh, but she couldn't think of a single word to say.

A few minutes later she walked beside Dan while he pushed the stroller with Allen in it. The girls ran on ahead, laughing and shouting.

"You're sure quiet today, Roxie."

"I know."

"How come?"

She shrugged.

Dan cleared his throat. "How's . . . how's Lacy?"

Roxie trembled. "Fine." She knew she should tell him the truth, but if she did, he'd hate her forever.

"Is she at work?"

"Yes."

"Does she tell you . . . things?"

"Never! Lacy acts like I'm not around most of the time."

"Oh."

Roxie peeked at him from under her dark lashes. He looked relieved. He was afraid Lacy had told her about his calls and the roses!

At the park the girls played in the sandbox, while Allen watched from his stroller. Several kids played ball, others whizzed down the slide, and two girls sat in the swings and talked.

Roxie sat on a green bench. Why had she agreed to come?

Dan sat beside her and watched a teenage boy and girl strolling along holding hands. He sighed heavily.

Roxie glanced at Dan, then quickly away. If she told him the truth, would he feel better?

"I'm thinking about finding my real dad and going to live with him."

Roxie's eyebrows shot up almost to her hairline. "You are?"

"I really don't want to stay in Middle Lake any longer."

"Does Mary know?"

"I was going to tell her, but I haven't yet."

Roxie helplessly shook her head. "But what will your family do without you?"

Dan shrugged. "They'll get along." He picked up the squeeze-toy Allen had dropped and held it out to him. "I'll miss 'em, of course."

"Please don't go, Dan."

He looked at her in surprise. "Why should you care?"

If only he knew! "You wouldn't be happy away from your family. And Mary would miss you a lot."

"I'd miss her too . . . and the others." Dan stabbed his fingers through his dark hair.

Silently Roxie prayed that Dan would make the right choice. She prayed for help to tell Dan the truth. She moistened her dry lips with the tip of her tongue. "Lacy doesn't know you sent the roses," she blurted out. "It was me you talked to on the phone . . . not Lacy. It was a terrible thing for me to do, and I'm really sorry."

Dan stared at her for a long time. Finally his face lit up, and he smiled. "Then she doesn't hate me?"

Roxie's heart sank to her feet as she shook her head. She was glad she'd told him the truth, but inside she felt like tears were drowning her heart.

"Did she like the roses?"

"Yes," Roxie whispered hoarsely.

"Then I don't have to leave Middle Lake! I'm going to see her and talk to her! Maybe she'll go to the Sunday school party with me next week."

Roxie bit back a cry of pain.

"Should I ask her?"

Roxie shrugged.

Dan caught Roxie's hand and squeezed it. "You're a good friend."

Roxie stared down at Dan's hand over hers. Shivers ran over her body. He took his hand away, and she wanted to grab it back.

"Thanks for helping me. And for helping Mary too. She sure needs you."

Roxie cupped her hand over the hand Dan had touched. She wanted to lock his touch away so she could keep it forever.

7

More Plans

Roxie rolled the last bite of the strawberry ice cream around on her tongue and let it slide down her throat. It was cold and creamy and delicious. She pushed the glass bowl toward the center of the kitchen table to give her room to prop her elbows on the table. Mom, wearing a pink blouse tucked in her jeans, and Dad, in his old blue shirt and faded overalls, sat across from her. Lacy and Eli were out for the evening, and Faye was already in bed asleep for the night. Roxie took a deep breath. She'd told Mom and Dad about the Harlands, but not the part about Dan and the roses. That was too embarrassing for her to talk about with them. "What can we do for Mary and her family?"

Dad chuckled. "I always said you were the greatest!" He reached over and rubbed Roxie's head gently.

She grinned and ducked back. She hated having her hair messed up, but she knew Dad was being loving, not mean.

Mom reached across the table and stroked Roxie's hand. "I'm proud of you, Roxann."

Roxie's stomach tightened. Grandma Potter always called her Roxann. She didn't want to think of Grandma Potter and her plans to marry Ezra Menski. So far Grandma hadn't said anything to them, but Roxie knew she would in time. Impatiently Roxie forced her mind back to the Harlands.

Dad folded his arms across the bib on his overalls. "I can fix the leaky faucet."

Mom chuckled. "I think Roxie means a little more help than that."

Dad sobered and nodded. "The biggest help we can give them is to teach them about Jesus. I know Ray Harland slightly, but I can get to know him better and then tell him God is his answer."

"And I can do the same for Angela. I've seen her in church, but I've never bothered to get acquainted." Mom sighed and shook her head. "We get so caught up with things that are important to us that we forget to look around at the walking wounded so we can help them." She flushed self-consciously. "I sure got carried away, didn't I?"

Roxie wasn't used to Mom and Dad talking about Jesus and helping others, but it felt good. No, it felt *great*.

Dad kissed Mom's cheek. "I'd rather get carried away than be like we were before." He smiled at Roxie. "You and your friends keep praying for the Harlands and keep helping them the best you can. Your mom and I will take care of what we can. Tell Mary to stay home with Allen and wait. God answers prayer!"

Smiling, Roxie nodded.

Mom leaned forward. "Mary shouldn't be in charge of those kids like she is. She's too young. I'll talk to some of my friends, and we'll see if we can't get some adults involved. Of course, what I'd like to see is Angela and Ray take the responsibility they should. And I believe they would if they didn't feel so overwhelmed."

A weight lifted off Roxie. It felt good to have Mom and Dad help with a problem that was too big for her alone.

The next morning before Sunday school Roxie stood just inside the Sunday school wing and told the Best Friends all that had happened. She didn't tell them about Dan and their talk in case anyone overheard, but she knew she'd tell them when they were all alone. Best Friends shared secrets—they shared everything! Later when Mary arrived, Roxie pulled her aside and excitedly told her help was on the way.

"Mom and Dad both said they'd do something."

"Thank you," Mary whispered with tears in her eyes.

After church Roxie saw Mom talking to Angela Harland. Roxie laughed right out loud. The plan was already being put in motion! She saw Dan talking to Lacy, and she turned quickly away. Lacy had another boy to add to her collection!

"Is anything wrong, Roxie?"

She gasped and looked up to find Rob McCrea, Chelsea's thirteen-year-old brother, standing there. Roxie smiled. She and Rob had become friends from almost the first day the McCreas had moved in next door. Now he wore a light blue dress shirt tucked into black dress pants. "Hi, Rob. I'm just feeling jealous of Lacy and Dan Harland."

"You're kidding!"

"I know it's dumb, but that's how I'm feeling anyway."

"I guess I get jealous once in a while. Like when Dad pays more attention to Mike than to me. Or when Nick Rand has more computer stuff than I do."

Roxie smiled. It wasn't quite the same, but she felt better just because Rob talked to her. "What do you do about it?"

Rob shrugged. "I asked Jesus to forgive me, and I pray a special blessing on Mike and on Nick."

Roxie's eyes widened. "I don't know if I could do that!"

Rob grinned. "Yeah, me either. But I do it anyway—with God's help."

Roxie smiled. It was nice to have Rob talk to her like that.

"Did Chelsea tell you about my new job?"

Roxie shook her head. "What is it?"

"Teaching computer to Ezra Menski!"

Roxie scowled. "That's dumb!"

"He wants to learn so he can keep better records." Rob chuckled. "I think he wants to play computer games with your grandma."

"Don't you dare say that!"

"Hey, I was only kidding." Rob looked at her closely. "What's wrong?"

"Nothing!"

Rob shrugged. "Anyway, I start tomorrow. It'll be kind of fun. And the pay is good."

Roxie wanted to tell him never to work for Ezra, but she closed her mouth and watched him run to his car.

Later, on her way to Chelsea's to meet with the Best Friends, she thought about Rob again. He was nice even though he was going to teach Ezra computer. Why couldn't her brother Eli be like Rob?

Hearing the girls talking and laughing in Chelsea's backyard, Roxie ran around the garage. The girls were sitting on a blanket on the ground in the shade of a maple tree. They were drinking iced tea from tall glasses.

"Hi, Roxie!" Chelsea handed a glass of iced tea to Roxie.

"Thanks." Roxie sank to the ground and took a long drink. Ice cubes clinked against the glass. Chelsea had brewed the tea and had put sugar in it. Roxie loved the taste.

Hannah held her glass between both her hands and leaned toward Roxie. "Tell us the rest of your story, Roxie. The part about Dan."

Her stomach tightened, but Roxie told them about her talk with Dan.

"Good for you!" Hannah and Kathy said together.

"I could never give away the boy I love." Chelsea shook her head. "Never! But you did a very nice thing, Roxie."

"Love means putting others first," Kathy said softly.

Roxie felt a little better.

Her face thoughtful, Hannah twisted a strand of hair around her finger. "Once I really really wanted a red and blue beaded necklace. I had enough money to pay for it, but that's all. Then I saw my sister Lena with a ring that she wanted. She'd lost a special ring she'd gotten for her ninth birthday, and she wanted another one. Well, she didn't have enough money to pay for the ring. I wanted her to have that ring." Hannah pulled her legs to her chin. "I put the beads back and helped

Lena buy the ring. She was so happy. And it made me feel good to do it."

Kathy cleared her throat. "Once I had one of those soft teddy bears that feel good to hug, and Megan wanted it. But I knew she'd sleep with it and slobber on it or drag it through the dirt. This was last year when she was three." Kathy bit her bottom lip and shivered. "I wouldn't give it to her, even when she cried. Mom and Dad said it was my decision. I still have the bear, but every time I look at it I think about how much Megan wanted it. I was too selfish to give it to her. I still feel bad."

"You could still give it to her," Roxie said.

Kathy shook her head. "It wouldn't be the same. Besides, she doesn't even want it now."

Chelsea had a faraway look in her eyes as she touched her *I'm A Best Friend* button. "Back in Oklahoma when I had Sidney for my best friend she wanted a special pair of pink socks I had, so I gave them to her because I wanted her to be happy." Chelsea's face clouded over. "She wore them once to school, then ran around in her driveway with them on without any shoes. She knew not to do it, but she did it anyway! She got big holes in them and couldn't ever wear them again. I loved those socks, and she ruined them! It made me feel terrible—but she was still my best friend. I didn't stop loving her just because she ruined my special pink socks."

"Giving up Dan is different than giving away a

pair of pink socks," Roxie whispered. "I wish Lacy wanted only pink socks, but she wants every boy around."

"Except Francis Lisser." Hannah giggled.

Roxie laughed and nodded. "I should give her Francis as a gift!"

"Wrapped in a red bow," Kathy said with a chuckle.

"I've never seen Francis Lisser." Chelsea looked at the girls. "Why doesn't Lacy like him?"

"Because he follows her around like a sick puppy," Roxie said. "And he's not very smart. Lacy is. She says it takes Francis all day to make up his mind about anything. Lacy makes up her mind in a second. He gets a D in everything, and she gets an A almost every time."

"Maybe we should all meet with Francis Lisser and teach him how to act around girls, how to study, and how to make quick decisions." Kathy nodded, and her eyes twinkled. "That's a great project for us!"

"Lacy would fall in love with him and leave Dan for you, Roxie," Chelsea said.

Roxie shook her head. "He likes me, but only like a sister. I know that. It hurts though. Besides, he's sixteen! I can't go out with boys until *I'm* sixteen. He'll be twenty by then. He sure won't wait that long."

Hannah shook her head. "I guess not. But my

grandma told me she loved Grandpa when she was twelve and he was eighteen. They got married when she turned sixteen."

Roxie gasped. "Sixteen! I would never get married then!"

"I'm not getting married until I'm thirty-five," Kathy said.

Chelsea sighed. "I want to get married right out of college, have three kids, then decide what I want for a career. Maybe photography."

Roxie rested her chin in her hands, her elbows on her knees. "Doesn't it seem like we will always be this age and always be in school? It's hard to imagine living in our own homes and having families of our own." She shivered. "It would be terrible to live like Mary Harland does."

"Or worse, live on the street," Kathy whispered. She twisted a blonde curl around her finger. "I wish we could take all the street people, find places for them to live, and get jobs for them. I cry sometimes when I see people living on the street."

"There are shelters," Hannah said. "Maybe we could give some of our *King's Kids* money to a shelter to help the homeless."

"That's a good idea." Chelsea narrowed her eyes thoughtfully. "How much is in the treasury, Hannah?"

"Around $10. We would've had more, but we

bought Pampers and a few baby things last month for that baby Kathy told us about."

"Ten dollars doesn't seem like much," Roxie said.

Hannah lifted her chin. "It's better than nothing. I vote we give it."

Chelsea lifted her hand. "Who votes yes?"

They all raised their hands.

"Good. Hannah, you take care of it."

"I will."

Roxie suddenly burst out laughing. "We always end up having a business meeting even when we only meet to talk."

Chelsea flung her arms wide and threw back her head. "That's because we're so wonderful!"

Roxie laughed with the others. How had she survived without her best friends? Until two months ago she'd never had a best friend. Now she had three! If she had a pair of pink socks, she'd give them to Chelsea right now. If she had red and blue beads, she'd give them to Hannah. If she had a soft teddy bear, she'd give it to Kathy so she wouldn't feel guilty when she looked at hers.

"Best friends forever!" they all shouted, then fell over giggling.

Roxie sat up and watched Chelsea, Hannah, and Kathy. Could anything ever happen that would break them up?

8

The Flower Contest Judges

Roxie stepped out in the yard where Mom and Faye stood looking at the flowers. She squinted in the hot morning sun. Excitement crackled in the air.

"Tomorrow's the day, Roxie!" Mom clasped her hands together. "I think I'm going to win the Prettiest Flowers Contest. Just look at the gorgeous blossoms!"

Faye bent down to smell one, then wrinkled her nose. "It stinks."

Roxie laughed. "They aren't judging them on the smell." She pointed to a tiny purple flower. "Smell that one. It smells sweet and perfumy like a flower should."

Faye squatted down and sniffed. "Ummm. It does smell good!"

Mom touched tall red zinnias and short yellow

marigolds. "I think I'll win again." She sighed. "Then again, there are lots of yards in The Ravines with beautiful flowers. I noticed how pretty the Shigwams' flowers are. Maybe they'll win."

Faye tugged on Mom's hand. "Can we go to the park now? You looked at the flowers twenty million times already."

Mom laughed. "All right, let's go. We'll be back later, Roxie."

"I'm going to Mary's for a while."

"Your dad and I were there yesterday."

"That's great." Roxie hugged Mom. "Thanks!"

"You're very welcome. We're going to continue to help however we can."

"Bye, Roxie." Faye waved. "Want to go with us?"

"Maybe another time." Roxie ran into the house for a drink of cold water before she went to Mary's. *A glass of Chelsea's iced tea sure would taste good right now,* she thought.

Roxie started for the door just as the phone rang. She was the only one home, so she answered it, even though she was sure it was for Lacy. It almost always was.

"Roxie, it's Dan Harland."

Roxie sagged against the kitchen counter. Dan! "Lacy's not home."

"I need to talk to you."

89

"Me?" Roxie's pulse leaped. "I was just on the way to help Mary."

"Could you stop by the flower shop? It's important."

Roxie frowned. "Sure. I'll see you in a few minutes."

"I'll watch for you and meet you outdoors."

Roxie slowly hung up the receiver. Was Dan going to ask her about Lacy? Roxie pressed her lips tightly together. Why had she even agreed to meet him? Maybe she'd just ride straight to Mary's. Roxie frowned. She couldn't do that. There was something in Dan's voice that scared her a little. Was he going to go live with his real dad after all?

A few minutes later Roxie stood beside her bike in the shade of Middle Lake Flower Shop. Exhaust fumes drifted across the street from the filling station. Her mouth was bone-dry—from the heat and from being nervous about talking with Dan.

He slipped out the side door of the shop and motioned for her to follow him to the back of the shop. He looked upset.

"Roxie, I didn't know who else to tell." Dan took a deep breath and wiped sweat off his forehead. "I know your mom wants to win the flower contest tomorrow."

"Yes." What was he getting at?

"Because you've been good to us, I had to tell you." Dan stuffed his hands deep into the pockets of his jeans. "Mrs. Peabody owns the flower shop, and she's one of the judges tomorrow for the contest."

"So?"

"She was talking to the other judges, and they all agreed Councilman Columbus should win. And, Roxie, they haven't even *looked* at the flowers yet! They said it would be good press for the councilman and for their businesses."

"That's awful! My mom is so sure she's going to win!"

"I know." Dan shrugged helplessly. "I can't do anything else, but maybe you can. You can't let anyone know I told you this. I'd lose my job for sure."

"I don't know what to do either, but thanks for telling me."

Dan nodded and grinned. "I owed you something." He started back to the door, then stopped. "I didn't have the nerve to tell Lacy I sent her the roses."

"Do you want me to tell her?" Roxie gasped. What was she saying?

Dan shook his head. "I'll do it. It's just that I'm afraid she'll hate me."

"I don't think she will. Did you ask her to go to the Sunday school party with you?"

"I couldn't. She's so smart and so pretty. Why would she go with me? I'm nobody!"

Roxie shook her finger at Dan. "Don't you dare

say that! You're wonderful!" Roxie turned crimson-red. "I mean . . . you shouldn't feel that way. Lacy likes boys who are smart and nice and don't walk after her like a sick pup."

"Like Francis Lisser does."

Roxie laughed. "Yes. How'd you know?"

"I've watched him. And I have to listen to him talk about Lacy all day long. I feel like filling his mouth with potting soil."

"But you won't."

Dan grinned sheepishly. "Guess not."

"Don't be jealous, though. And pray a special blessing on Francis." Roxie couldn't believe she'd actually said that. But she was glad she had.

"You're a good kid, Roxie."

She blushed. "Thanks for telling me about the judges. I don't know what to do, but I'll think of something." She wheeled her bike along the side of the flower shop. She stopped and looked back at Dan. "Don't be afraid of Lacy. If she turns you down, so what? At least you've tried."

"I guess."

Roxie smiled, then pedaled away. She stopped at Chelsea's to call a special meeting. Soon the Best Friends were sitting in Chelsea's kitchen drinking iced tea. Roxie quickly told them what Dan had told her.

"It's really no big deal," Hannah said with a

shrug. "I heard them say last year they wished they could've given the award to *my* mom."

"Why couldn't they?"

"Because we're Ottawa. They said the others would be angry if we won."

Roxie wrinkled her brow. "That's terrible! Now this year no one has a chance because they want the councilman to win."

"They should get different judges," Chelsea said, spreading her hands wide.

"Of course!" Kathy nodded. "The committee that asked the judges to be judges can tell them not to be. Who's on the committee?"

"Matty Rowlings is. And she lives across the street from Ezra Menski. Let's talk to her right now!" Roxie swallowed the last of her tea and started for the door.

"Will she even believe us?" Chelsea asked.

Roxie sighed heavily. "Probably not."

"But Ezra will," Hannah said with a firm nod. "We'll tell him, and he can tell Matty Rowlings."

Roxie didn't want to see or talk to Ezra, but she knew it was the only way. "Remember, we can't say a word about Dan or he'll lose his job. Hannah, you do the talking since Ezra likes you best."

Several minutes later the girls stood on Ezra's porch while he sat in his glider and listened to Hannah. Gracie lay behind the glider, her head on her paws. While he listened, Ezra sipped ice water through a straw in the huge glass in his hands. The glider creaked as he moved.

"So, will you talk to Matty Rowlings?" Hannah asked.

Ezra was quiet a long time. Finally he eased himself up and leaned on his cane. His green plaid shirt and gray pants hung loose on his frame. "She might not do anything at this late date, but I'll have a talk with her anyway. I'm pleased you girls are concerned enough to do something about those judges. Not everybody would." He looked right at Roxie.

She fell back a step, her cheeks rosy. "It was my idea!"

"Did I say it wasn't?" Ezra walked carefully down the steps. "I'll let you know what happens. Don't wait around here. It might take me a while to get Matty to do something."

"Call me when you know, and I'll tell the others." Hannah smiled, and Ezra smiled back.

Roxie knotted her fists. He would never marry Grandma Potter if she had anything to say about it!

Later at her house Roxie told the Best Friends good-bye, and she straddled her bike and rode to Mary's house. Mary's mom, Angela, answered the door. She looked too young to be the mother of so many children. She wore white shorts and a pale pink T-shirt. Her long fingernails were painted a bright pink.

"So you're Roxie Shoulders!" Smiling, Angela patted Roxie on the back. "I talked to your mom Sunday, and she and your dad came over yesterday. They're real nice."

"Thanks." Roxie carefully stepped around Allen, who was sitting on the floor tearing up a newspaper.

The three little girls turned from watching TV and said, "Hi, Roxie. Want to read to us?"

"Sure. Later maybe."

Mary stepped out of the kitchen. "Hi, Roxie. Come see what I've done."

"She's doing a real good job with her painting. I didn't know my girl had it in her." Angela laughed, then bent to pick Allen up off the floor. "You girls go on to the kitchen."

Roxie hurried to the kitchen. It felt strange having Angela there.

Mary looked rested, and her eyes lit up as she smiled. "I'm almost finished, thanks to you." Mary held the canvas out to Roxie.

Standing so the sunlight shone through the window on the painting, Roxie studied the rosebud. Her heart almost stopped beating when she saw how beautiful the painting was. A wave of jealousy washed over her, leaving her weak and trembling. Her picture was still unfinished and not nearly as good as Mary's.

Mary took the canvas back with a troubled frown. "Don't you like it?"

Roxie wanted to say it was the worst work she'd ever seen in her life, but she remembered her talk with Rob about jealousy. Silently she asked Jesus to forgive her, then prayed that Mary could finish the painting to look as good as what was already done. Roxie finally smiled. "It's absolutely beautiful, Mary!"

"Really?"

"You're a great artist!"

"Thanks to you." Mary brushed away a tear. "I couldn't have done any of it without you."

"I'm glad I could help." Roxie looked around. The sink was empty, the faucet didn't leak, and the floor was swept. "I guess there's nothing for me to do today."

"Your mom and dad were here. They're nice. Your dad even went to see Ray." Mary bit her lip. "Maybe they won't get a divorce after all."

"Aren't you glad?"

"Only if Ray gets a job. He's mean when he's out of work."

"My dad will help all he can."

"I know. Roxie, I never knew what it was like to have folks who cared about us and helped us. I'll never forget you."

"Not even when you're a famous artist?"

"Not even then!"

Roxie talked and laughed a while longer with Mary, said good-bye to her and her family, then rode home. Maybe Ezra had called Hannah with news about the judges.

Roxie wheeled her bike into her yard and saw Ezra Menski standing outside the garage, his cap in his bony hand. Roxie wanted to turn and pedal away fast. But she put her bike away and walked over to Ezra. "Hello," she said hesitantly.

"You got me all wrong, Roxann."

Roxie froze. "About what?"

"I don't hate you. I like you. You got brains and guts and talent. So quit thinking I hate you."

Roxie rubbed her hands up and down her arms. She didn't know what to say.

"Matty said she'd find new judges. She was sure angry to hear what was going on. This time she'll get folks who won't be persuaded to cheat."

"Thank you for helping. Did you tell Hannah?"

"Sure did. I was on my way home when I spotted you coming, so I thought I'd tell you in person . . . and get this thing settled between us."

Roxie didn't know if it was settled or not, but she didn't say anything. She moved from one foot to the other. "I don't hate you either," she blurted out. "But you can't marry Grandma Potter."

Ezra straightened up and glared down at

Roxie. "You can't be telling me what I can or can't do! I'll marry her if I want. And I want!"

"She has a husband! Grandpa Potter."

"He's gone, and so is my wife. Emma and I are free to get married to each other. That's that!" Ezra thumped his cane on the sidewalk, then walked away, his head high and his back stiff.

Roxie whimpered and shook her head. She heard Hannah calling to her. She forced back thoughts of Ezra and Grandma Potter and ran to meet Hannah.

The next day Roxie waited in her yard with Mom, Dad, and Faye as the judges—three women and two men—walked up and down the sidewalk, admiring the flowers and writing on papers on their clipboards. The sun was bright but not too hot. For once even Faye stood quietly. Roxie felt Mom's tension. What would happen if Mom didn't win? She wanted to more than anything. The judges would visit the home of the winner at five o'clock, take pictures, then have a big write-up in tomorrow's newspaper. The winner would be awarded a plaque on a stake that would be pushed into the ground near a flower bed. In the fall the winner could unhook the plaque from the stake and hang it on a wall inside the house. Roxie knew Mom wanted to see the plaque near her flowers and later on her wall.

Finally the judges walked on down the street, and Roxie heard Mom blow out her breath.

"I don't know if I can wait until 5." Mom took Dad's arm and walked toward the house.

Faye ran after them and tugged on Mom's blouse. "Will you cry if you lose?"

Mom bent down to Faye and kissed her cheek. "No, I won't cry."

Dad smiled at Mom. "She'll be happy she has beautiful flowers to look at even if the judges decide on another yard of flowers."

Roxie watched Mom's face. She was having a struggle to agree with that. But finally she smiled, and Roxie relaxed.

"Winning is nice, but I can handle not winning too."

Faye ran back to Roxie. "Can you handle not winning the rosebud contest?"

Roxie bit her lip. "I don't know, Faye."

Dad squeezed Roxie's shoulder, "Sure you can, Roxie. Our help comes from God."

Faye flipped back her ponytails. "Yup, that's right."

Roxie thought about that and nodded. Not winning would be hard, but she'd survive.

Later at five o'clock the judges rang the doorbell. Roxie raced Faye to the door, but Mom beat them both. The whole family crowded around the door. Mom's face glowed as she accepted the award. Lacy and Eli clapped and cheered as loudly as Faye did.

"Congratulations!" the judges said.

Almost bursting with pride, Roxie followed them to the yard and stayed off to one side, but the photographer told her to stand with her family. She stood in front of Dad and beside Faye. While the photographer clicked pictures, the Best Friends ran into the yard. As soon as she could, Roxie ran to them.

"Mom won." Roxie smiled at Chelsea. "You should be really proud since you helped with the flowers."

Chelsea nodded, then whispered, "I told Mom I'd make her a flower garden next year. So watch out, Mrs. Shoulders!"

Roxie grinned. She knew Mom could handle it.

"We should call Dan and let him know," Hannah said.

"Let's do!" Chelsea cried.

Kathy caught Roxie's arm. "I think we should do something special for Dan . . . like talk Lacy into going to the Sunday school party with him."

Roxie pressed her hand to her heart. Could she do that? Blood roared in her ears as she followed the Best Friends to Chelsea's house.

9

Roxie's Terrible Plan

Roxie took a deep breath as she stopped outside Lacy's bedroom door. Yesterday she'd agreed to do her part to get Lacy to go with Dan to the party. Oh, why had she agreed? She knew it was because the Best Friends had talked her into it. Even Chelsea had said she should since Dan had helped make the flower contest honest. He'd been happy to learn what had happened.

Eli walked out of his room wearing his gray running shorts and short-sleeved shirt. His short dark hair needed brushing, and his sneakers were untied. He pushed his glasses up against his face and frowned at Roxie. "Did you see my big white T-shirt?"

"No."

"If you do, make sure you don't wear it."

"Why would I wear it?"

Eli raked his fingers through his dark hair.

"Who knows? Why does any girl do what she does?"

Roxie suddenly felt sorry for Eli. She took a step toward him. "What girl do you have in mind?"

Eli flushed. "What do you care?"

"I don't know." Roxie walked right up to Eli. It felt funny having a conversation with him. "What girl?"

He hesitated a while, then shrugged. "Janine Belisle."

"Do I know her?"

"She lives beside Mrs. Rowlings."

"Oh, yeah! I know her. She used to baby-sit for the Shigwams."

"Right."

"She's nice."

Eli rolled his eyes. "This last month she's been running in the park the same time as me. But she won't even talk to me."

"Do you talk to her?"

"Of course not. I don't want her to tell me to leave her alone."

Roxie smiled and felt very grown-up. "She probably started running the same time as you so you'd talk to her. She's kind of shy, you know. So be brave and talk to her."

"What about?"

Roxie thought about the Best Friends' rules for making friends. "Ask her about herself. Find out if she's running because she wants to be in track or for exercise or just for fun. Ask her what classes in school she likes best." Roxie spread her hands wide. "Ask her about herself. And about her family. If she's too shy to ask you about yourself, tell her a little. Once you start talking together, it should be easy to keep talking."

Eli smiled. "Thanks! You're pretty smart for a kid."

"I'm only three years younger than you."

"Like I said, a kid." He grinned and headed for the stairs. "If you see my big white T-shirt, toss it on my bed, will you?"

"Sure." Roxie smiled and walked back down the hall. Maybe if she followed the rules of making friends with Lacy and Eli, they might stop ignoring her.

Taking a deep breath, Roxie knocked on Lacy's door. Lacy's music was turned up loud, and the smell of her perfume was strong even with the door shut. "Lacy, it's me."

"I'm getting ready for work," Lacy shouted over the music.

"Can I talk to you?"

"Oh, all right."

Roxie opened the door and stepped inside. The big room was in perfect order. Lacy stood in front of the full-length mirror, looking at the yellow dress she wore. She spun a little, and the dress swirled out from her slender legs. A long yellow clip held back her auburn hair. "You look nice, Lacy."

"Thanks. What did you want to talk about?" With her eyes narrowed, Lacy stood with her hands on her waist. "You'd better not want me to baby-sit Faye tonight. It's your turn!"

"Don't worry. I'll watch Faye." Roxie wanted to walk out. Why should she do anything nice for Lacy? Actually she was doing it for Dan anyway—not for Lacy! That kept her from storming away. "There's a boy who really really likes you."

Lacy smiled and turned her music off. The silence was abrupt. "Oh? Who?"

Roxie's heart turned over. How could she do this? "Dan Harland."

Lacy's eyes lit up. "I thought so!"

"Would you go to the Sunday school party with him?"

"If he asks me, I might."

"Why can't you be sure?"

"It depends on how he acts. If he acts like a scared rabbit like Francis Lisser, then I'd say no so fast he'd be even more afraid to ask me again." Lacy stamped her foot. "I can't stand scaredy-cats!"

"Dan's nice, and I think you should be patient with him. Help him ask you."

"No! No way! If he can't be man enough on his own, tough!"

Roxie knotted her fists. "That's mean, Lacy."

"Too bad! Get out and let me finish getting ready."

Roxie rushed to the door, then turned back, her eyes flashing. "Dan is nice. He works hard, and he's smart. He thinks you're too pretty and too smart for him."

Lacy smiled. "He does?"

"But I'm going to tell him to stay away from you. He's too good for you!"

"Hey, don't you dare talk to me like that!"

Roxie slammed the door, ran to her room, and slammed her door. Her chest rose and fell. "She doesn't deserve Dan! I hope Francis Lisser hangs around her forever!"

Suddenly an idea popped into Roxie's head that was more brilliant than any she'd had in her entire life. Why not talk Francis into giving Lacy a rose? She'd think he'd given her the other roses too. Oh, it would be pure joy to see the look on Lacy's face if she thought Francis had sent the roses!

Roxie raced downstairs and pedaled to the flower shop. She couldn't stop to think about her plan or she might back out. She left her bike at the side of the shop and ran up the steps and into the store. The bell tinkled. Smells of flowers and potting soil hit Roxie hard and almost took away her breath.

Francis stood at the cash register waiting on a woman who was buying a huge crystal vase.

Roxie's heart hammered so loudly she thought Francis could hear it. She walked slowly around, looking at the vases and potted plants and then the flowers in the huge refrigerated display case. The minute the woman walked out, Roxie dashed over to the counter.

"Hi, Francis." Oh, but it was hard to breathe!

"Hi, Roxie." Francis turned pink all over. "How is your sister Lacy today?"

"She's fine." Roxie leaned on the counter and lowered her voice almost to a whisper. "I think it would be very nice of you to send her a red rose. She loves red roses."

Francis ran a finger around the neck of his white T-shirt. "I could do that."

"You could even write her a note on this card." Roxie pulled a card just like the one on the first rose and dropped it between Francis and herself.

"What would I say?"

Roxie screwed up her face as if she were thinking really hard. "'Lacy, I know you like roses. Here's one from a dozen. Love, Francis.'"

"Oh, I don't know."

"Come on, Francis. Be bold! That's what Lacy likes . . . bold, forward boys." Roxie glanced toward the door that led to the back room. "Is Dan Harland here today?"

Francis nodded.

"He'd be brave enough to send Lacy flowers."

Francis lifted his weak chin. "Then so am I."
He bent over the card and wrote exactly what Roxie
had said to write, put it in a tiny white envelope, and
printed LACY SHOULDERS on it. He strode to the display case and took out one long red rosebud and a
green fern. He wrapped green paper around both,
stapled it all shut, and stapled the card to it. "Here!
Take this to Lacy. I'll stop by and see her after
work."

"She'll be gone. But you could come tomorrow
at your lunch break. You could even have lunch
with her!"

Francis almost broke his face with his wide
smile. "Thanks, Roxie. I won't forget this."

Roxie grabbed up the wrapped rose and darted
out of the store. She pedaled home in a frenzy and
raced inside. Lacy was ready to walk out the door
to go to work. "Look what came for you, Lacy!"
Roxie thrust the wrapped rose into Lacy's arms.

Lacy smiled. "Oh my, another one! This is so
romantic!" She tore back the paper and smelled the
rosebud, then slowly pulled the card from the tiny
white envelope.

Roxie's stomach tightened. She could barely
stand still.

Lacy's face fell, and she flung the card down.
"It *was* Francis all along! Oh, I hate roses!" She ran
out the door, the car keys clutched in her hand.

Roxie picked up the card and the rose and

laughed. "You got just what you deserved, Lacy Shoulders! Wait'll I tell the girls!"

A few minutes later Roxie sat in Hannah's basement bedroom on her bed and told her every detail of what she'd done. Chelsea and Kathy were both working *King's Kids* jobs and couldn't come. "Lacy is mean. I can't wait to see her face tomorrow when Francis shows up for lunch!"

Hannah pulled her legs against her chest. "Poor Francis. He'll feel terrible when he sees Lacy doesn't want him around."

Roxie chewed on her bottom lip. "I guess I didn't stop to think about Francis."

"I'm not trying to make you feel bad, Roxie, but did you forget you want to love others like Jesus loves them? Trying to hurt Lacy isn't loving her."

Suddenly Roxie could see just what she'd done. It wasn't funny or nice. It was mean and cruel. Roxie's shoulders slumped, and giant tears welled up in her eyes. "Oh, Hannah, I don't think I can ever learn. I am so sorry!" Roxie rocked back and forth and moaned. "It's too late to undo what I did. When will I learn?"

Hannah patted Roxie's arm. "We'll think of something."

"But what? Will I have to tell Francis what I did?"

Hannah nodded.

"Oh, noooo!"

"But I'll go with you if you want." Hannah scooted off the bed and hooked on her sandals. "Ready?"

Roxie pressed her hands to her hot cheeks. "Oh, I don't know! How can I face Francis? How can I ever tell Lacy what I did?" Roxie threw up her hands and let them fall to her sides. "It's better to *stay out of* trouble than *get into* it, isn't it?"

"Sure is. Mom says it'll take our whole lives to learn that."

"I hope not." With a deep sigh Roxie walked outdoors with Hannah.

Several minutes later they stepped inside the flower shop. Mrs. Peabody stood at the counter. Roxie cleared her throat. "I need to talk to Francis Lisser for a minute."

"I'm sorry, but he went home already."

"Oh no." Roxie looked helplessly at Hannah.

"Could you give us his phone number so we can call him?" Hannah asked.

"Sorry. I don't give out the phone numbers of my employees."

With her head down Roxie walked out of the shop. She stopped at the bottom of the steps and looked at Hannah. "He's going to show up for lunch tomorrow. What'll I do?"

"We'll call him when we get home. We can get his number from the phone book."

Roxie laughed in relief.

The minute she reached home Roxie ran to the kitchen phone. She smelled the spice potpourri Mom had on the counter as she opened the phone book for Francis's number. She ran her finger up and down the Ls. "I can't find a Lisser listed!"

Hannah took the book and looked. "It's not there. Call Information."

Roxie did, but they had no listing for a Lisser either. "Oh dear! Oh dear, oh dear!"

Hannah slowly slipped the phone book back into the drawer. She leaned her elbows on the counter and rested her chin in her hands. Finally she straightened up and smiled. "We'll just have to wait for him outdoors and stop him from coming inside tomorrow."

"Yes! That's exactly what we'll do!"

Hannah slapped her forehead. "But I can't! I have to baby-sit tomorrow from 10 in the morning until 3 in the afternoon."

"I can't do this alone, Hannah. What about Chelsea and Kathy?"

"They have jobs again tomorrow."

Roxie's heart sank. How could she face Francis all by herself and tell him what she'd done?

10

Francis Lisser

Roxie paced her yard, staying in the shade as much as possible. It was almost too hot to breathe. She rubbed her sweaty hands down her yellow shorts and tugged at the neck of her T-shirt. She'd tried to call Francis at the flower shop, but Mrs. Peabody had said he'd gone out to deliver flowers and wouldn't be back until after lunch.

"What'll I do? What'll I do?" Roxie wrung her hands. She had had all kinds of conversations with Francis inside her head, but what would she say to him face to face? She'd prayed for the words, and she knew the Best Friends were praying for her too. So far her head was totally empty of the right thing to say.

With a ragged sigh Roxie glanced at the house. Lacy was helping Mom and Faye fix lunch. Roxie bit her lip. She hadn't found the courage to tell Lacy what she'd done or that Francis was coming for lunch. What a mess she'd gotten into just because of her anger at Lacy!

Just then Dan Harland rode his bike into the driveway. Roxie froze, and icy chills ran over her. Then she broke out in a sweat.

"Hi, Roxie." Dan wiped sweat off his face. "It's sure hot."

"Dan! What a surprise." The worst surprise in the entire world!

"I decided to come see Lacy during my lunch break. Today I'll ask her to the party." Dan nodded firmly and looked very determined.

Roxie glanced around wildly. Was Francis in sight yet? She turned back to Dan and grabbed his hand. "You have to leave right now! I've done the worst thing in the world!"

Dan looked at her strangely. "What's wrong?"

"I was mad at Lacy, and I actually told Francis Lisser to come for lunch to ask Lacy out."

"Roxie! I can't believe you'd do that to your own sister."

"I know. She deserved it, but I shouldn't have done it." Roxie heard a high-pitched cry of a motor. She looked toward the street. Francis was driving toward them on a minibike. Roxie yanked Dan behind a tall bush. "What'll I do? I can't hurt Francis's feelings."

Dan sighed heavily. "I guess I can talk to Lacy later."

"Oh, thank you, thank you, thank you!" Roxie squeezed Dan's hand.

"It's all right." Dan laughed and pulled his hand free.

"I'll tell you how to ask Lacy so she'll go out with you." Roxie took a deep breath. "Act toward her just like you do to me. You know—nice and not shy. Tell her you'd like her to go to the party with you. Tell her you sent her roses twice, but you wish you would've handed them to her yourself."

"Thanks, Roxie. I'll do it. I hate it when I get shy."

"It's only because you're afraid of what she'll say to you. So what if she says no? Will you drop over dead?" Roxie shook her head hard. "You can find someone else to go with you if Lacy says no."

"You'd better get out there. Francis stopped outside your garage." Dan chuckled and pushed Roxie away. "Let me know what happens."

"I will." Roxie trembled, squared her shoulders, and walked toward Francis. He wore tan dress pants and a white short-sleeved shirt with a striped tie. He looked nervous and frightened. Roxie wanted to hide, but she smiled and waved. "Hi, Francis."

"Hi, Roxie." His voice broke. "I came for lunch."

"So I see." She twisted her fingers together. "This isn't going to be easy."

HILDA STAHL

"What?"

"Can I talk to you before you go in?"

He nodded. "Did I do something wrong?"

"No . . . I did." She led him around the house to the picnic table and asked him to sit down. "Francis, I was mad at Lacy yesterday, and I did a really, really terrible thing."

"I always took you for a nice kid."

"Well, not always, that's for sure." How she hated to admit that! "Sit down." She sat beside him on the wooden bench in the shade of a maple and told him what she'd done and why. He looked ready to faint. "I really didn't think about how this would hurt you until it was too late. I'm sorry. I'm really really sorry."

Francis rubbed his jaw and looked ready to cry. "I knew it was too good to be true. Why would Lacy ever go with me? I know I make her mad, but I just can't help it."

"Sure, you can. Lacy's only a girl. Sure, she's pretty and she's smart, but she's only a girl—not a goddess. Don't fall all over her, and don't act like she's some beautiful princess."

"But she is one!"

Roxie shook her head. "She's nice part of the time and rude and mean part of the time. She's an ordinary person. You know she's not nice to you."

"But it's my fault!"

"No, it's hers, because she can't stand shy peo-

114

ple. She likes a person to speak up and take control." Roxie picked up a leaf that had fallen to the table and tried to balance it with her finger. "Lacy doesn't even know you're coming to lunch. If she did, she'd leave." Roxie touched Francis's thin arm. "I'm sorry. If you want to leave, you can."

He tugged his tie loose and unbuttoned the top button of his shirt.

"If you want to stay, I'll tell the family the truth—I *did* invite you for lunch."

Francis smiled weakly. "I'm hungry. Why not stay?"

"Good! And remember, don't be afraid of Lacy."

"That'll be pretty hard."

"Pretend she's me ... or some other girl you're not shy with."

"I'll try. If I start acting shy or afraid, kick my leg and I'll try to stop."

"It's a deal." Roxie pulled his tie. "Take that off, would you? This is only lunch, you know."

Francis stuffed his tie into his pants pocket. "I hate ties, but I thought Lacy would be impressed."

"She wouldn't." Roxie jumped up. "Are you ready?"

"I guess."

Roxie's legs trembled, but she forced them to support her as she walked to the house and through the back door with Francis. She smelled toast and tuna. "Mom, I brought company for lunch," she called to warn them.

Francis stopped short, sweat breaking out across his forehead. "I've got to get out of here."

"No!" Roxie whispered, pulling on his thin arm. "Come on—I promise you won't faint."

"I don't know about that."

"Take a deep breath."

Francis breathed deeply.

"Let it out."

He did. "I'm ready," he whispered hoarsely.

Roxie led him to the kitchen. Lacy had her head in the refrigerator. Faye already sat at the table chewing on a carrot stick. Mom stood at the counter, cutting sandwiches in half. "Mom, I asked Francis to come for lunch today."

Mom shot Roxie a puzzled look, then smiled at Francis. "Hello, Francis."

Lacy spun around, her face white. She didn't say a word.

"Hi, Lacy," Francis said with a smile.

"Hello," she finally said.

"I'll get out another plate." Roxie hurried to the cupboard and pulled out a plate, glass, silverware, and napkin. She set them on the table in Eli's place and motioned for Francis to sit down. Lacy never said another word, but Mom and Faye talked to Francis and made him feel welcome. As they ate tuna sandwiches, a fruit salad, carrot sticks, and potato chips and drank lemonade Mom got Francis to talk about working at the flower shop. He told interesting stories about some of the customers and some of the strange flower arrangements he'd been asked to make.

Roxie felt Lacy's eyes boring into her, and she could barely taste her food. She finally glanced at Lacy, then looked again. Lacy was actually listening to Francis and smiling!

"I want to work in a flower shop when I grow up," Faye said.

Roxie chuckled. Faye picked a new career at least twice a day.

"How do you like your job, Lacy?" Francis asked.

Roxie held her breath to see how Lacy would answer.

"I like it. And I get a big discount on clothes. I already have my school clothes."

Roxie breathed a sigh of relief and took a big bite of sandwich.

Francis took a drink of lemonade, then set the glass back in place. "Lacy, are you working on the yearbook this year?"

Lacy nodded. "Are you?"

"Yes."

Roxie hid a smile. Francis was doing okay. He looked at her and grinned. She nodded to reassure him.

After lunch Francis said, "Thanks for the delicious lunch. I have to get back to work now." He walked to the door, and Roxie followed him. "Bye." He smiled right at Lacy where she still sat at the table. "See you around."

"See ya," Lacy said.

"Bye," Faye and Mom both said.

"Thanks for asking me, Roxie."

She nodded.

He walked out, closing the door with a tiny snap. Roxie breathed a sigh of relief. It was over, and it had been okay!

Lacy jumped up and gripped Roxie's arm. "How could you do that to me? How could you?"

Roxie jerked free and rubbed her arm.

"Calm down, Lacy," Mom said sternly. "He's a nice boy." Mom frowned. "Don't act like a snob. You're not one—not really."

Roxie disagreed but didn't say anything. She sat on her chair and moved her napkin around with her finger.

Mom walked around to Faye. "Let's get you down for your nap."

"Nap? Mom, I am starting school in September. Remember?"

"I remember. Right now it's your nap time." Mom walked out with Faye pulling on her hand.

Lacy glared at Roxie. "I can't believe you did that!"

"I'm sorry."

Lacy burst into tears and dropped back on her chair. "I was so embarrassed! Imagine! Francis Lisser here!"

"Lacy, I'm sorry. I asked Francis to come just to get even with you."

Lacy lifted her head and her eyes snapped. "I knew it!"

"But I'm sorry. I tried to stop Francis, but it was too late. I told him what I'd done, and he wanted to come to lunch anyway. He didn't hang all over you, Lacy."

"He *was* fun to listen to," Lacy said reluctantly.

"I really am sorry for trying to get even with you. Honest."

Lacy sighed. "I was a brat. I'm sorry too."

Roxie gasped in surprise. She'd never heard Lacy say she was sorry. "You really should make friends with Francis. He's nice."

"I guess he is."

"So is Dan Harland."

Lacy nodded. "I know."

"Give him a chance to ask you to the party, Lacy."

"What does it matter to you?"

"He's nice, and I like him." Roxie shrugged. "I want him to be happy." She couldn't say she owed Dan a favor or that love always put another person first. "So, will you be patient with him and let him ask you out?"

Lacy sighed heavily. "I suppose so." She jumped up. "I have to get ready for work."

Roxie leaned back in relief and silently thanked God for helping her. Maybe now she could keep her mind on her painting and finish the picture for the contest.

Another Job for Roxie

Roxie helplessly shook her head as she listened to Mary say her painting was too terrible to turn in for the contest. "How can you even say that, Mary! Just look at it!"

Mary looked at it and flipped it over on the table. "It'll be the worst one in the contest."

Roxie knew better. Kathy's would be the very worst. "You were pleased with it yesterday. What made you change your mind?"

"I have to turn it in! What will Zelda Tandee think of it? What will the judges think? I can't take a chance, Roxie . . . I just can't!"

Roxie sighed and leaned back on the kitchen chair. "Mary, don't get scared now. The deadline is in three days. Your picture is already done. Take it in today and forget about it."

"You don't understand, Roxie. I put my whole heart into that! What if nobody likes it?"

"You won't know if you hide it in your bedroom, will you? You have to take a chance." Roxie jumped up, suddenly impatient. "Mary, I came here to help you so you could get your painting done. How can you say my help was all for nothing? That's not fair to me!"

Mary hung her head. "I know."

"Come on! We're going to hand in your painting this very morning. You said your mom would be home soon. When she gets here, we'll leave."

"All right," Mary whispered. Her face lit up. "Do you really think it's good enough to turn in?"

"Yes. I really do, Mary."

A little while later Mary handed her painting to Zelda Tandee while Roxie stood at her side. Roxie saw Mary's hand tremble, and she heard the tremor in her voice, but she wouldn't let Mary lose her nerve. While Mary filled in the contest entrance form, Roxie slowly walked down the line of paintings already on exhibit for the contest. One side of the store was full of books and papers. Pencils, paintbrushes, and other small items filled a glass case. The smell of paint was strong in the air. Roxie studied each painting carefully. Her pulse fluttered, and she smiled. She had a very good chance to win. But so did Mary. Clay Ross hadn't turned in his painting yet. Roxie's fingers itched to get back to work on hers. Just a little more time on it and she'd be done and could turn it in. She wouldn't have any trouble meeting the deadline.

A few minutes later Roxie walked outdoors with Mary.

"I'm so glad you made me bring my painting!" Mary grabbed Roxie's hand and pumped it up and down. "Mine is better than a lot of them, isn't it?"

Roxie nodded. "I told you you were good."

Mary sobered. "Roxie, what if I beat you?"

"Then you do." Roxie bit her lip. "Not everybody can win. I want to, but so do you. So do the others. I can survive if I don't win."

"I don't know if I can."

"Sure, you can. You'll always have your painting, and you'll keep on painting no matter what happens. You plan to be a famous artist, right?"

"Right!"

"So don't let anything make you quit—not even losing a contest." Roxie was talking to herself as well as Mary.

The next day Roxie stood in the basement and carefully put the last details on her painting. She'd turn it in tomorrow. Finally she stood back and studied the picture. A long-stemmed red rosebud nestled inside a white florist box on a green lacy fern. A tall white vase stood beside the box, and they both sat on a red bunched-up cloth. Her heart swelled with pride. She'd done a better job than she'd thought she would. "It's good," she whispered. "It's really good."

She cleaned her brushes and put everything in order, then slowly walked up the basement stairs. It felt as if she'd left a part of her behind.

"Roxie, come here quick." Eli stood in the hallway and beckoned to Roxie.

She saw the excitement on his face as she hurried to his side. He smelled sweaty from just returning from his run. "What's up?"

"I finally talked to Janine! I did just what you said, and it worked!"

"Good."

Eli grinned self-consciously. "I didn't think it would, but I decided to do it anyway." He pushed his glasses up on his face. "It was better than doing nothing."

"Did you run with her today?"

Eli nodded. "And we're going to run every day, even after school starts. She wants to be in track. Last year she didn't make the team, but this year she's determined to make it. I told her all the stuff I know about training."

Roxie wanted to leap high and shout for joy. She was having a conversation with Eli! He didn't think she was a bothersome little sister any longer! When he finished talking about Janine and running, Roxie said, "Want to see my painting for the contest?"

"Sure. Well, maybe later. I've got to hit the shower, then mow the lawn." Eli ran upstairs.

Roxie sighed. Would he really look at her work? She shrugged. If he didn't today, maybe he would tomorrow.

Roxie ran to her room and changed into her jeans and an old T-shirt. Today she had to clean Teresa Bongarr's garage. Chelsea had assigned the job to her yesterday afternoon. It was only a block away, and thankfully today wasn't as hot as it had been. Mrs. Bongarr was a sixty-five-year-old widow, and nobody liked working for her. So whenever she called for someone, Chelsea drew a name from a hat. Roxie wrinkled her nose. Her name had been drawn this time. She ran downstairs and poked her head into the living room where Mom was reading to Faye. "I'm going to work now. I'll be back for dinner."

"Don't let Mrs. Bongarr take advantage of you," Mom said. "If she gives you too much to do, tell her she'll have to hire someone to help you."

"I will."

Faye jumped up, her eyes sparkling. "I could do it! I'm big!"

"Sorry, Faye." Roxie smiled. "You have to be nine or older."

Faye plopped back on the couch with her arms folded and a pout on her face. "It takes too long to get old! Why wasn't I born sooner so I'd be older?"

Mom laughed and pulled Faye close. "You were born at just the right time, honey. Why, you're already four! You were only three last year."

Roxie chuckled as she hurried outdoors. She stopped short. Lacy and Dan stood in the yard, talking and laughing. "Hi," Roxie said stiffly.

"I'm going to the party with Dan tomorrow night, Roxie."

"Thanks to you," Dan said, smiling at Roxie. "I told Lacy how much help you gave me."

Roxie bit her lip. It was hard to let go of her feelings for Dan.

"Thanks, Roxie," Lacy said softly.

Roxie stepped back in surprise. "You're welcome," she managed to say. Lacy had said thanks! Roxie said good-bye and ran down the street to Mrs. Bongarr's. She was standing in her yard talking to Ezra Menski. Roxie frowned. What was he doing talking to Mrs. Bongarr in such a friendly manner? Didn't he really love Grandma Potter after all?

"Hello, Mrs. Bongarr." Roxie smiled. She barely nodded at Ezra. "I'm here to clean your garage."

"I'll be right with you." Mrs. Bongarr turned back to Ezra. "I will be glad to go with you tomorrow. But it'll have to be after 7."

"That's fine. I'll pick you up."

"I'm looking forward to it."

Ezra barely nodded to Roxie. "Tomorrow after 7, Teresa." He leaned on his cane as he slowly walked away.

Mrs. Bongarr sighed heavily. She rested her hands on her waist and watched him walk away. "He's a fine catch. Any woman would be glad to be his wife."

Roxie rolled her eyes.

"Well, let's get you to work, shall we? Come inside, and I'll show you what I want you to do."

"You told Chelsea I was to clean the garage."

"First I want you to unload my kitchen cupboards, so I can wash them and repaper the shelves." Mrs. Bongarr walked toward the back door. Her denim skirt flapped around her skinny legs. She wore white socks and white sneakers.

Roxie followed Mrs. Bongarr to the kitchen. It smelled liked coffee and burned toast. All the doors for the cupboards that lined the walls hung open. A stepladder stood beside the table.

"Stack the dishes and other things on the table, floor, and countertops. Just don't break anything." Mrs. Bongarr filled a red plastic utility bucket with soapy water. "Start on the top shelves and work down, Roxie. I have a few bottom shelves already unloaded. I'll start washing those."

Roxie carried the stepladder to the first cupboard and climbed up as Mrs. Bongarr turned on the radio. Classical piano music blasted into the room.

"I like music when I work," she shouted over the music. "If you need to get my attention, just yell."

Roxie forced back a groan as she climbed the ladder. For the next hour she unloaded cupboards. Then Mrs. Bongarr asked her to help wash and repaper them.

"You can do the garage tomorrow," she shouted.

"Will you pay me for both?" Roxie hated to ask, but she knew she had to. Chelsea had said never to work without being paid unless they agreed ahead of time to do the job as a good deed. Work for Mrs. Bongarr was never to be a good deed because she always took advantage of them.

Mrs. Bongarr frowned, then finally nodded. "Of course I'll pay you for both. Now get to work. I won't pay you for doing nothing."

Three hours later Roxie walked wearily home. Her head ached from the loud music. Her muscles ached from climbing up and down the ladder a million times. She'd clean the garage tomorrow and then tell Chelsea she'd never work for Mrs. Bongarr again.

Roxie slowly walked into her house. The cool air felt good against her hot body. She dragged into the kitchen, where Mom and Grandma Potter sat having lemonade.

"Roxann! You look terrible!" Grandma rushed to Roxie's side and slipped an arm around her. "What have you been doing?"

"Working for Teresa Bongarr," Mom said before Roxie could answer.

Grandma turned white, dropped her arm, and sat back down. "Why her?"

"She needed help." Roxie saw the startled look on Grandma's face and wondered about it. She filled a glass with lemonade and sat at the table. "Ezra was there talking to her."

Grandma swallowed hard. "Oh?"

"What's wrong, Mother?" Mom asked.

"Nothing, Ilene." Grandma jumped up. "I've got to get home. I'll call you." She rushed out, grabbing her purse as she hurried out the back door.

"That's strange," Mom said.

Roxie drank half her glass of lemonade in one gulp. It was tart and icy-cold and felt good on her throat. She set the glass down. "Ezra and Mrs. Bongarr are going out tomorrow night after 7."

Mom's eyes widened. "You don't say!"

"She's really excited about it. She says he'd make any woman a fine husband."

Mom twisted her glass and frowned thoughtfully. "I wonder if Grandma is jealous."

"Jealous?" Roxie laughed and shook her head. "Why should she be?"

"I know she likes Ezra more than she's saying."

Roxie bit her lip to keep from blurting out what Ezra and Grandma had said about marriage when she was spying. Maybe she didn't have to worry about them getting married after all. Maybe Ezra would marry Mrs. Bongarr.

Roxie laughed under her breath. If he did, he'd be working from morning 'til night.

Just then Roxie thought about how upset Grandma had been. Would she be hurt badly if Ezra married Mrs. Bongarr?

Roxie finished her lemonade and set the glass in the sink. What could she do to make Grandma feel better? Maybe she could call her and talk to her about her painting. Grandma always liked to talk about art. It made her think about Grandpa.

Roxie smiled as she slowly walked to her room.

12

The Deadline

Yawning, Roxie pulled on her jeans and her old T-shirt. She had to get to Mrs. Bongarr's. "How could I sleep so late?" Roxie frowned at her clock, then rolled her eyes. She'd forgotten to set her alarm last night.

She ran to the kitchen for a quick breakfast. Mom was just heading out the door with Faye.

"Don't forget to turn in your painting, Roxie. See you at noon."

"Bye," Roxie mumbled, but Mom and Faye were already gone. Yawning, Roxie pulled the box of Kix off the shelf, dumped some in a bowl, and poured milk over it. Suddenly she lifted her head. *What did Mom say? The deadline! I have to get my painting in this morning!*

She ran to the basement, grabbed the picture, and raced back to the kitchen. Maybe Grandma Potter would turn it in for her. Roxie grabbed the phone and called Grandma's house. The phone rang and rang. It had last night too when she'd tried to call. Roxie slammed down the receiver just as someone knocked on her back door. She ran to answer it. It was Chelsea. "Am I ever glad to see you!"

Chelsea laughed. "Why?"

Roxie led her to the kitchen and told her about Mrs. Bongarr, then about the deadline. "So, will you please *please* take it in? I already filled in the entry form, so you only have to hand it in. Before noon, Chelsea."

"Sure. Okay." Chelsea studied the painting. "It's really good, Roxie."

"Thanks." Roxie stuffed a spoonful of Kix into her mouth.

"You'll probably win, won't you?"

Roxie nodded as she chewed. She found a bag and stuck the stretched canvas inside. "I'm glad you stopped over, Chel."

"Yeah, me too." Chelsea held the bag to her. "Did I tell you I talked to Clay Ross?"

"No! When?" Roxie ate while Chelsea talked about Clay.

"I think he's beginning to like me." Chelsea sounded wistful. "I told him I'd do anything for him." She flushed. "I guess I'd better go. See you later."

"Okay. And, Chel, make sure I never have to work for Mrs. Bongarr again!"

"I'll try." Chelsea walked out with Roxie's painting tight against her chest.

A few minutes later Roxie knocked on Mrs. Bongarr's door. Roxie waited and knocked again. She couldn't hear any sounds from inside the house. She pressed the doorbell and heard the chimes. "Where is she?" Roxie walked slowly around the house. Mrs. Bongarr hadn't paid her yesterday. She said she wouldn't give her a dime until the whole job was done. Had she gone away just so she wouldn't have to pay?

Roxie walked all the way around the house. Mrs. Bongarr wasn't there. "I should go home right now and forget about being paid!" But she rang the doorbell twice more and knocked again. With a loud sigh she started down the sidewalk. Suddenly a car stopped at the curb, and Mrs. Bongarr climbed out. Ezra Menski was driving the car!

Roxie's stomach knotted. Ezra had taken Mrs. Bongarr out twice! What would Grandma Potter think?

Ezra drove away without waving.

Mrs. Bongarr hurried to the garage door. She wore a blue dress and matching blue sandals. "I see you're right on time, Roxie. I want all the tools picked up and put away, a few boxes straightened, and the floor swept and washed down. Try to be done by noon. I'm going somewhere with Ezra again."

Roxie pressed her lips tightly together. Grandma Potter wouldn't like this at all. With a sigh Roxie started to work, while Mrs. Bongarr hurried inside her house. Cleaning the garage wasn't hard; it just took a lot of time. She sneezed as she swept. Later she sprayed the floor with the hose. Icy water splashed back on her. Was making money really worth all this work? She thought about the two new sweaters she'd bought for school and nodded. The sweaters hadn't been in Mom and Dad's budget for school clothes, and if she hadn't worked, she wouldn't have been able to buy them.

But now that she had the sweaters, maybe she'd stop working for *King's Kids* and just stay home. It would seem strange to have all the free time she wanted to hang out at the mall or with the Best Friends. Roxie turned off the water and coiled the hose back in place. Then again, if she didn't work and the Best Friends did, she wouldn't have anyone to hang out with.

Roxie stood in the open doors of the garage and checked to make sure she'd done everything. The garage looked clean and tidy. She chuckled. "I'm done! I'm done and I'm never coming back," she whispered. She didn't dare say it aloud in case Mrs. Bongarr was within hearing.

Roxie ran to the back door and knocked.

Mrs. Bongarr flung open the door and frowned. "What is it? I'm very busy."

"I finished the garage, and I'm ready to go. You can pay me now."

"Oh, all right. I really should dock your pay though."

"Why?"

"You put a shelf paper on crooked yesterday." Mrs. Bongarr rummaged around in her purse and finally pulled out the pay they'd agreed on. "You tell the kids in the *King's Kids* they need to work harder for less pay."

Roxie pushed the money into her jeans. "Have fun with Ezra today."

"I surely will!"

Roxie said good-bye and slowly walked home. In the kitchen she tried to call Grandma Potter again. There was still no answer.

After lunch Roxie walked listlessly outdoors. It felt strange not to be doing something. Usually she'd be helping Mary work on her painting or baby-sitting Faye or doing a *King's Kids* job. This afternoon she didn't have anything to do. She could read. There was a book she'd started and never finished.

Slowly she walked from her yard into Chelsea's. Maybe Rob would be home. Chelsea had said she'd be gone. Just then Roxie heard voices from around the house. Smiling, she ran around the garage, then stopped short. Chelsea and Clay Ross were standing in the backyard talking together! Clay wore a green-striped shirt tucked into new jeans.

Chelsea wore lilac-colored shorts and a T-shirt with balloons on the front.

"Hi," Roxie said as she walked toward them.

They jumped apart. Chelsea's face was red and Clay's white.

"What?" Roxie asked with a frown as she looked from one to the other.

"I have to go." Clay ran away as if his sneakers were on fire.

"What's wrong?" Roxie frowned after Clay, then turned back to Chelsea. She looked ready to faint. "What's wrong?"

"Who says anything's wrong?" Chelsea snapped. "How come you're here? You were supposed to work for Mrs. Bongarr."

"I already finished, and she paid me."

"Oh. Well, I don't have time to talk right now."

"Do you have a job this afternoon?"

"No . . . But I have things to do."

"I could help you."

Chelsea shook her head, and her long red hair swished across her back. "I don't need help. Gotta go. See ya."

Strange chills ran up and down Roxie's spine as she watched Chelsea run into her house. "What's wrong with her?"

Roxie dashed across the street to Hannah's house. Maybe she'd know. Roxie rang the doorbell, but no one answered. It was strange to have all the

Shigwams gone. With her shoulders slumped Roxie walked back home.

In the kitchen she called Kathy, but her brother Duke said she had gone shopping with her mom and Megan.

Roxie poured a glass of orange juice and drank it. She looked in the refrigerator to see if anything interesting was there. The shelves were almost empty. Eli must've gone through the leftovers again. She closed the refrigerator and walked to the window. Birds pecked at something in the grass and then flew up into the trees. She thought about Grandma Potter and tried calling her again. There was still no answer.

Suddenly the phone rang. Roxie jumped, giggled, and answered it. It was Talease Fowler, a girl from her class.

"Roxie, I saw your painting at Tandee's."

"You did?" Roxie smiled with pride.

"It wasn't quite your usual kind of work, do you think?"

"I'm getting better."

"Oh . . . Well, I just thought I'd call. See ya next month in school."

Roxie hung up with a puzzled frown. Why would Talease call just to say that? They weren't friends or anything.

The phone rang again, and Roxie jumped again. She answered hesitantly. Was it Talease calling back to say something more? But it wasn't Talease. It was Ginger Richardson.

"Roxie, I saw your painting at Tandee's."

"Oh?" Roxie frowned. How strange.

"It's . . . ahhh . . . different."

"I do paint better than I did last year. I've been practicing."

"Actually, I thought last year's work was better."

"You did?" What was going on here?

"I'd better go. I just wanted to ask you about your strange painting."

Roxie hung up slowly. "Strange painting? What did she mean by that?"

The phone rang again, and she snatched it up and practically shouted, "Hello."

"Roxie?"

"Yes."

"It's me . . . Tammie Boyer."

Tammie Boyer? Never in her life had she called Roxie before. "Hi, Tammie."

"I saw your painting at Tandee's."

"What in the world is going on? Talease and Ginger called too."

"I guess they told you."

"Told me what?"

"Oh." Tammie was quiet a long time.

"Told me what?" Roxie's stomach fluttered nervously. "Told me what, Tammie?"

"About your painting."

"What about it?"

"Go look at it yourself."

"Tammie, I painted it! I already saw it!"

"Oh . . . Okay . . . See ya in school."

Frowning, Roxie hung up. Just what was going on? Maybe she *should* go look at her painting. Maybe Zelda Tandee had hung it upside-down or sideways. It wasn't like her to do that, but maybe she had.

Roxie raced outdoors, grabbed her bike, and pedaled to the art supply store. Her face was wet with sweat, and nervous chills ran down her back. She pushed open the heavy plate-glass door and stepped inside. The air was cool and dried her damp skin.

"Roxie Shoulders!" Frowning, Zelda Tandee hurried toward her with her hands in the wide pockets of her red, blue, and green smock. Her dyed brown hair was pulled back in a bun, and blue eye makeup made her blue eyes seem large in her oval face. "I'm surprised you didn't care enough about this contest to do your best work."

Roxie stared at Mrs. Tandee as if she were speaking a foreign language.

"The others did what I expected. But not you, Roxie. Not you. You really disappointed me."

Roxie's legs trembled, and she couldn't speak around the lump in her throat.

"If you came to take it back, it's too late. The deadline is past, and what's in stays in." Mrs. Tandee brushed a piece of lint off her black slacks. "I'm sorry."

Roxie bit her bottom lip and moved restlessly. "Let me look at my painting," she said hoarsely.

Mrs. Tandee frowned, sending deep lines from the corners of her eyes to her hairline. "It's hanging with the others." She led the way. "See? That's why I'm disappointed with you."

Roxie stared at the painting. Ugly leaves in a strange shade of green lined the long stem of her beautiful rosebud. The room spun. "But I didn't . . . I didn't paint those leaves!"

"Now, Roxie, don't tell me you think someone else would do that to you."

Roxie nodded, her eyes burning with tears. She'd given her painting to Chelsea to turn in. Would Chelsea do this to her? No! Never! But Clay Ross might—so he would win. The idea hit Roxie so hard she stumbled back. "I've got to go."

She pedaled to Chelsea's as fast as she could go. Maybe Chelsea had given the painting to Clay—she would if he asked her to. She'd do anything to make him like her. And once he got it, he could've painted the ugly leaves on it.

Roxie dropped her bike in Chelsea's yard and raced to the door. She knocked, then knocked again. She caught a movement at the window and glanced over in time to see Chelsea peeking out. Chelsea jumped back and let the curtain fall in place.

"Chelsea, open the door! Now!"

"Go away, Roxie! I don't want to see you right now."

Roxie pounded on the door so hard that pain shot up her arm. "Open the door, Chelsea!" Roxie rattled the knob. The door was locked or she would've gone on in to face Chelsea.

"I saw the painting!" Roxie shouted.

Chelsea didn't answer.

"I trusted you!"

Still Chelsea didn't answer.

After a long time Roxie picked up her bike and slowly walked home. Chelsea had ruined her chance of winning the contest. But even worse—Chelsea had ruined their friendship.

Roxie closed her eyes and moaned.

13

Chelsea

Anger boiling inside her, Roxie sat in her yard with her back against a maple tree and watched both Hannah's house and Chelsea's. "I worked so hard on it," she muttered over and over. "How could Chelsea let Clay Ross spoil it?" But Roxie knew the answer. Chelsea had said she'd do *anything* to make Clay like her.

Roxie covered her face with her hands. "She hates me. Chelsea McCrea hates me."

Just then a car drove past and then slowed down. Roxie jumped up. The Shigwams were home! She dashed across the street, calling to Hannah as she climbed from the brown Ford station wagon.

Hannah ran to her and caught her arm. "What's wrong? Did somebody die?"

Roxie tried to speak but couldn't. Finally she gasped out, "Chelsea let Clay Ross paint ugly leaves on my painting for the contest. It's hanging up in the store for everybody to see! There's not a single chance for me to win."

Helplessly Hannah shook her head. "Chelsea wouldn't do that. There has to be another explanation. Let's go talk to her."

"She won't talk to me. She acted very guilty. She won't even open her door and let me in!"

"She'll talk to *me*." Hannah looked sure of herself—and very determined. "I know she will."

They ran across the street together to the McCreas'. At the door Hannah said, "Let me talk to her alone, okay?"

Reluctantly Roxie nodded, then slowly walked to her yard. Bees buzzed around the pretty flowers. A black squirrel raced across the yard and zipped up a tree just as Hannah ran back to Roxie . Her face was red, and she looked ready to cry.

"She won't talk to me either!" Hannah clamped her hand over her mouth, and her dark eyes grew big and round and frightened.

"I knew it!" Roxie slapped her leg. "She's guilty, and she's afraid to face us."

"It's not like Chelsea to do anything wrong."

"Ha! That's a laugh! She made that big phone bill and tried to keep it from her parents."

"I forgot about that."

"She's not perfect just because she's from Oklahoma, you know."

Hannah sighed. "I love her! We have to help her!"

Roxie almost choked. "Help her? What about *me*?"

Hannah sank back against a tree and sighed heavily. "I know she hurt you and made it impossible for you to win the contest, but think how much *she's* hurting. She's feeling guilty and frightened. And she probably thinks we won't ever love her again."

"Well, she's sure right about that!"

"No, Roxie, no We are best friends forever—no matter what. Remember?"

Roxie flung herself down on the lawn and beat her fists against the grass. Finally she sat up and wrapped her arms around her legs. "This is really really awful."

Hannah dropped down beside her. "Let's get Kathy so when Chelsea's mom gets home she'll let us in to talk to Chelsea."

"I thought Kathy's painting was going to be the very worst in the contest, but mine is! Do you know how humiliating that is?"

"I know. I'm sorry." Sighing, Hannah stood up and brushed off her shorts. "Shall we call from your place or mine?"

"I'm going to wait right here in case Chelsea comes out of her house. You do what you want."

"Then I'll go home and call Kathy." Hannah

twisted her fingers together. "Roxie, please don't stay angry at Chelsea. Forgive her, and pray she'll forgive herself."

"Yeah, sure." Roxie laughed dryly. "Who cares if she ever forgives herself. And I sure won't forgive her! It's asking too much!"

"Oh, Roxie, please don't be that way. Jesus says to forgive. Remember? You said you wanted to stay out of trouble so you wouldn't have to *get out* once you're in."

Roxie covered her ears and shook her head. "I'm not going to listen to you, Hannah!"

"Oh, all right!" Hannah ran across the street to her house.

Slowly Roxie walked to the tree where she'd sat before to keep watch. She sank to the grass and leaned back against the rough bark of the tree. A red pickup drove by. Two girls on bikes pedaled past, laughing together. Another girl was riding a bike fast and almost collided with the two girls. Then that girl wheeled into Roxie's driveway and dropped her bike. It was Mary Harland! She looked ready to explode.

Roxie jumped up. "Mary! What's wrong? Did something terrible happen?"

Mary's chest rose and fell as she caught Roxie's hand. "I saw your painting at Tandee's! Oh, Roxie! Who would do such a terrible thing? Mrs. Tandee thought you'd done it, but I told her there was no way. Who did it?"

Roxie opened her mouth to tell on Chelsea, but the words wouldn't come out. It was one thing to tell Hannah, but another to tell Mary. "I can't tell you," Roxie whispered.

Mary bit her lip. Her round face was red and wet with sweat. "I knew you'd be kind and forgiving! I knew it!" Mary flung out her arms and beamed. "You're that kind of girl. You do just what God wants you to."

Roxie wanted to sink out of sight. How wrong Mary was!

"You helped me, and you even helped Dan. That was so sweet of you." Mary squeezed Roxie's hand again. "Thanks to you, Mom and Ray got help too. They're not going to get a divorce. Instead, they're going to work together on their marriage. Mom is even learning how to be a better mother from a woman at church." Mary's eyes filled with tears. "All because of you, Roxie—because you did what Jesus wanted you to do."

Roxie's heart melted, and she blinked back tears. She did want to do what Jesus wanted! But could she forgive Chelsea and forget about her anger? Yes! She not only could, she would—because Jesus said to. Chelsea was more important than a contest! Roxie swallowed hard. She could forgive Chelsea, but could she pray for her so she could forgive herself? Roxie struggled with the answer and finally gave herself to what she knew was right. Silently she prayed for Chelsea.

"I'm really sorry someone messed up your art, but I'm glad you're handling it okay." Mary smiled. "I've got to get back home, but I wanted to see you to make sure you really were okay. I don't want you hurt—ever!"

They talked a while longer, then said good-bye. Roxie stood under the tree and watched Mary pedal away. Roxie smiled. The agony she'd been suffering was gone! Just as Mary rounded the corner Hannah ran back, her black hair flying out behind her.

"I got Kathy, and she'll be here as soon as possible."

"Good." Roxie took a deep breath and told Hannah about Mary's visit and about her decision to forgive Chelsea.

"That's great." Hannah brushed away a tear. "Let's sit down and wait for Kathy."

Roxie sank to the ground and watched Chelsea's house. "I could be wrong, you know."

"About what?"

"Chelsea letting Clay Ross ruin my picture. Maybe she gave it to someone else to take in, and maybe that person ruined it."

"Maybe." But Hannah didn't sound very sure.

Several minutes later Kathy rode up. She left her bike beside the garage and ran to join Roxie and

Hannah. She looked hot and concerned. Her short blonde curls were damp with sweat. Her red shorts and white top looked clean and neat. "Did you talk to her yet?"

"No."

"But Roxie decided to forgive her."

Kathy smiled as she sank down beside Roxie. "I almost didn't get to come. Duke was practicing guitar with Brody and didn't want to watch Megan." Kathy wrinkled her nose. "You'd think Brody lived at our house as much as he's there. Don't get me wrong. I'm glad Mom and Dad are being like foster parents to him since his mom is always working, but it's sure hard to have him always there. Brothers! Sometimes they're not worth having."

"Eli actually thanked me for telling him how to talk to Janine." Roxie smiled. "It felt good. I did ask him if he'd look at my painting, and he said he couldn't right then, but he didn't tell me to get lost. I think he'll start acting like a brother should."

Hannah plucked at the grass. "I sometimes wish I had a big brother. Being the oldest is all right, but sometimes I hate it. And to have all girls except for the baby is really hard."

Just then Billie McCrea, Chelsea's mom, drove in with Mike. Roxie leaped up with Hannah and Kathy beside her. They ran to the station wagon before Mrs. McCrea could get out of the car.

"We need to talk to Chelsea," Roxie said breathlessly.

Mrs. McCrea glanced toward the house. "She should be home."

"She is." Hannah bit her lip. "But she's upset and wouldn't let us in."

"Could you convince her to see us?" Kathy asked softly.

Mike ran toward the house and shouted over his shoulder, "I'll tell her."

"Come inside and have a glass of iced tea, girls."

Roxie looked at Hannah and Kathy. They shrugged. "We'll wait for her around back at the picnic table if that's all right with you."

"Sure. That's fine. I'll send her out." Billie McCrea hurried to the house, leaving a faint whiff of perfume behind.

Roxie led the way around the house. She sat on the table with her chin in her hands, while Hannah and Kathy dropped to the grass under the tree.

A picture of her ruined painting flashed across Roxie's mind, and she trembled. This was probably the hardest thing she'd ever done in the world. She looked toward the house and waited for Chelsea.

14

Another Rosebud

Roxie heard the McCreas' door open, and she jumped to her feet. Hannah and Kathy leaped up beside her. Together they watched Chelsea walk slowly toward them, her face a red blob and her eyes swollen from crying.

Hannah ran to Chelsea and slid her arm around her. "Don't be scared. Roxie forgives you. We all love you. Tell us what happened."

Without saying a word Roxie reached out and squeezed Chelsea's hand. She squeezed back.

Her chin almost on her chest, Chelsea sank cross-legged to the grass under the tree, and the girls all sat in a circle, knees touching knees. Finally Chelsea looked at Roxie with wide, guilt-filled eyes. "I'm soooo sorry!"

"I know," Roxie whispered.

Chelsea took a long shuddering breath. A squirrel chattered in a nearby treetop. The smell of hamburgers grilling drifted across the yard. "I was on my way to hand in your picture, and I saw Clay Ross." Chelsea laced her fingers together. "He came right up to me, and he actually smiled at me. It was a beautiful dream come true."

"'I heard you tell Lorraine you were taking Roxie's picture in,'" he said. "'Could I see it?' I said sure and pulled it out of the bag and let him look at it. I was proud of it. 'It's good, isn't it, Clay?' I said, and he said, 'Yes.' He acted funny, kind of nervous, you know. 'She's going to win and I'm not!' he said kind of sadlike. That made me feel terrible. I wanted Clay to win more than anything. Sorry, Roxie. I'm just telling you how I felt.

"So I said, 'Clay, you're the best artist I know!' And he is good! But then he said, 'If I don't win, my dad will be disappointed in me. He says I should give up art and be like my brother and get into sports. I like sports, but I am an artist and I want to paint. If I win, my dad might start being proud of me as an artist.' So I told him, 'Well, I'm proud of you.' Clay leaned close to me and whispered, 'If you make sure I win, I'll be your boyfriend.'

"Well, you all know I'd do *anything* to make him go with me. I looked at the painting, and just like that I knew what I could do. I showed Clay how I could paint ugly leaves up and down the stem. He was really impressed at my idea. So . . . I took it back home, painted leaves on it, and took it to Tandee's."

Roxie groaned. "Chelsea, I thought Clay Ross painted on the leaves. But you did it! Oh, Chelsea!"

"I know! I'm mean, and I don't deserve for you to forgive me."

Roxie struggled with that a while. "I already forgave you."

"I hated myself the minute I handed it in and realized how it would look to the judges and to you." Chelsea dashed away a tear from her red lashes. "Clay was happy. He even walked me home. He said he'd hold my hand. But I couldn't stand to have him touch me. He used me! But even worse, I let him!"

"Now it's over," Roxie said.

"I hate Clay Ross!" Chelsea's chin quivered. "And I hate myself."

"You can't," Hannah said firmly. "When Jesus forgives you and you forgive yourself, you must stop hating yourself."

Kathy nodded. "That's right. And you can't hate Clay."

Roxie wanted to cut Clay's painting into little pieces, but she didn't say that, and she forced herself to quit thinking it. Jesus wouldn't cut up Clay's picture, so neither would she.

Two days later in the noisy crowd at Tandee's, Roxie pressed tightly against the Best Friends and waited for Zelda Tandee to announce the winners. Roxie saw Mary and Dan a few feet away. Mary looked nervous. His face white, Clay Ross stood close to Zelda Tandee. She wore a bright paisley smock over an orange blouse and orange slacks.

Zelda Tandee raised her hand high and called, "Quiet please. I have the winners' names here in my hand." She held up a piece of paper.

Roxie felt Hannah stiffen and glanced over at her. She looked nervous. Did she think she might win? Roxie had looked at Hannah's picture, but she couldn't recall how she'd felt about it. She'd been too wrapped up in her own work.

When the crowd grew silent, Zelda Tandee said, "I'll announce the first place winner first, then the second, then the third. After that I'll hand out the prizes—first place $50, second $25, and third $10. The three winners will leave their work on display for six weeks."

Roxie saw Mary grip Dan's wrist. Clay Ross pushed his hands deep into the pockets of his jeans.

"The first place winner is . . . Mary Harland!"

Mary gasped and turned as white as the paper in Zelda Tandee's hand.

Roxie clapped, but only a few others joined in. She knew Mary wasn't well-known like Clay or herself.

"The second place winner is . . . Clay Ross."

Clay shouted, "Yes!"

The crowd roared and clapped, and somebody whistled. Roxie clapped, but she saw Chelsea didn't.

"The third place winner is . . . Hannah Shigwam."

Hannah gasped and gripped Roxie's arm so hard it hurt.

Everyone clapped, Chelsea and Kathy the hardest. Roxie couldn't pull free from Hannah to clap.

"I can't believe it! I just can't believe it!" Hannah cried.

"Congratulations," Roxie said, and she meant it from the depth of her heart.

Later Roxie carried her painting home in a bag. Kathy and Chelsea walked beside her with theirs. Hannah's picture remained on display in the store. She'd painted a single red rosebud against a bright white background. One drop of water glistened on a leaf. Roxie could see how she'd won.

Roxie lifted the bag that held her picture. "I'm glad to get this hidden away until I can paint over the leaves."

"Are you sure you can fix it?" Chelsea asked with a worried look.

"Sure."

"I'm soooo glad!"

Roxie turned to Hannah. "Wait'll your family hears you won!"

Hannah beamed with pride. "I didn't think I stood a chance." She flushed. "Until you were out of the running, Roxie."

"You might've beat out Clay Ross," Chelsea said.

Hannah laughed. "No. I know he's better than me. But it's the first time I ever won anything!"

"Congratulations!" the Best Friends said for the tenth time, then laughed happily.

At her house Roxie told her family about the outcome of the contest, left her painting in the basement, then ran to her room to change into her blue shorts and white T-shirt. She'd agreed to meet the Best Friends in an hour to have a special celebration party for Hannah at Chelsea's house. Roxie brushed her hair and pinned on her *I'm A Best Friend* button.

Faye poked her head in the door. "Roxie, Mom says to come downstairs. Grandma Potter's here."

Roxie frowned thoughtfully. She'd been trying to talk to Grandma for the past few days. Was she here to tell them she hated Ezra and never wanted to speak to him again?

In the living room Grandma Potter sat in the rocker. She wore peach-colored dress slacks and a matching blouse. She looked nervous.

"Hi, Grandma." Roxie kissed Grandma's soft cheek and smelled her delicate perfume.

"Grandma has something to tell us," Mom said. She sat on the couch with Lacy and Faye. Eli sat on the floor and Dad on the chair that was *his* chair.

Roxie sank to the floor beside Eli. This was a family meeting, so that meant this was serious business.

Grandma cleared her throat and gripped the arms of the rocking chair. "I want all of you to be happy for me when I tell you my news."

Roxie locked her hands together as she darted a look at Mom. Her cheeks were flushed pink, and it looked like she was going to say something, but she didn't.

"You all know I've been seeing Ezra Menski."

Roxie bit her lip. Had Grandma learned about Ezra going out with Teresa Bongarr?

"Ezra and I have decided to get married."

Roxie gasped, and Mom cried out, then was quiet.

"Congratulations!" Dad jumped up and kissed Grandma. "We want only the best for you."

"Yes, we do," Mom said weakly.

"I'm happy for you, Grandma," Lacy said, smiling.

Faye bounced up and down. "Me too."

"What about Teresa Bongarr?" Roxie asked sharply.

Grandma smiled. "Teresa has been making the wedding arrangements for us."

"So that's it," Mom cried.

Roxie's eyes widened in surprise.

Grandma held up her hand. "We didn't want

any fuss. We want to have everything organized without a bother. This should be a time to enjoy—not a time to run ourselves ragged."

"And when is the wedding?" Mom asked stiffly.

"September first."

"What?" Mom jumped up, her face ashen.

Dad caught Mom close. "You want your mom to be happy, Ilene. Remember that. It's her life."

Mom nodded, then slowly knelt down beside the rocking chair and pulled Grandma close. "I love you, Mom."

Roxie waited for the anger to rise in her, but none did. She knew Grandma was happy, and that's all that mattered.

"Does this mean Gracie is in our family now?" Faye asked.

"I suppose," Lacy said with a chuckle.

"And Ezra will be our grandpa." Eli grinned. "Grandpa Ezra Menski. Sounds strange, doesn't it?"

"You'll get used to it," Dad said.

Roxie listened to all the plans for the wedding, starting with a family dress-up dinner next Sunday night when Ezra and Grandma would officially announce their engagement.

As they talked, the doorbell rang. Roxie ran to answer it. She opened the door, but no one was there. She frowned, then looked down. She shook her head and sighed. A long-stemmed red rosebud lay there with a card hooked to it. "Another rose for Lacy," Roxie muttered as she carefully picked up the rose so it wouldn't prick her. She glanced at the card, then looked closer. ROXIE SHOULDERS was printed on the card! The rosebud was for her! Who would've sent it? She stepped outdoors and closed the door. She didn't want her family to see her rose before she found out who'd sent it. She opened the tiny white envelope and read, "Roxie, you're the best." It wasn't signed. Who thought she was "the best"?

Roxie glanced around the yard. No one was in sight. Had Francis Lisser brought it as a joke? She'd seen him a few minutes yesterday, and he'd told her he had asked Melissa Lesco out and she'd said yes. He was happy, and he said Melissa was too.

Roxie sniffed the rose. The sweet aroma tickled her nose. Dan Harland wouldn't bring her a rose. He was too busy spending time with Lacy. They'd gone out three times already.

Suddenly the Best Friends jumped out from behind the bushes and shouted, "Roxie, you're the best!"

Roxie burst out laughing and ran to the girls. "Did you give this to me?"

"Yes!" they yelled in unison.

Roxie held the rosebud high. "I'll bring this

rose to our celebration, and it'll be for all of us. Best friends forever!"

"Forever!" they shouted together.

Roxie held the rosebud to her nose and sniffed. As long as she lived, whenever she smelled a rose she'd think of Hannah, Chelsea, and Kathy—her best friends.

You are invited to become a *Best Friends Member!*

In becoming a member you'll receive a club membership card with your name on the front and a list of the Best Friends and their favorite Bible verses on the back along with a space for your favorite Scripture. You'll also receive a colorful, 2-inch, specially-made I'M A BEST FRIEND button and a write-up about the author, Hilda Stahl, with her autograph. As a bonus you'll get an occasional newsletter about the upcoming BEST FRIENDS books.

All you need to do is mail your NAME, ADDRESS (printed neatly, please), AGE and $3.00 for postage and handling to:

BEST FRIENDS
P.O. Box 96
Freeport, MI 49325

WELCOME TO THE CLUB!

(Authorized by the author, Hilda Stahl)